THE
DOUBLECROSS

(And Other Skills I Learned as a Superspy)

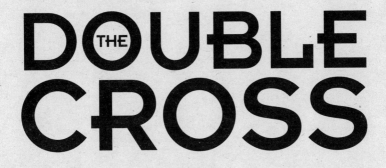

THE DOUBLE CROSS

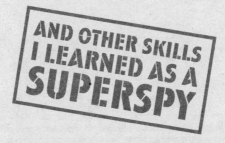

AND OTHER SKILLS I LEARNED AS A SUPERSPY

JACKSON PEARCE

SCHOLASTIC INC.

ISBN 978-1-338-03483-7

12 11 10 9 8 7 6 5 4 3 2 1   16 17 18 19 20 21

Printed in the U.S.A.   40

First Scholastic printing, March 2016

Book design by Nicole Gastonguay
Typeset by Westchester Book Composition

For Grandaddy,
real-life crime fighter

THE
DOUBLECROSS

(And Other Skills I Learned as a Superspy)

CHAPTER ONE

I should make one thing clear, right off the bat: *It. Wasn't. Cheating.*

Agent Otter, who is the exact opposite of a cute and chirpy water mammal, said, and I quote: "Whoever crosses the finish line first doesn't have to do pushups at the end of afternoon training." Do you know how many pushups I can do? *Zero*. Well, no, wait—I can do half of *one*. Because I can definitely get down; I just can't push myself back up, which is maybe the more important half of the exercise.

The finish line was the double door leading into the dining hall. The track—if you could call it that—wove through the halls of Sub Rosa Society headquarters. Upstairs. Downstairs. Past the wall of "windows"—glass panels with lights that were supposed to make us forget we were six stories underground. I wasn't sure exactly how long the track actually was, but it *felt* like twenty-five, maybe thirty miles. Every week for the past four years of my life, I ran it. And every week, without fail, I came in last place.

Not just by a hair, either. Last, as in "most of my classmates had already changed out of their training clothes by the time I crossed the finish line" place. This always gave them plenty of time to line up and laugh at me when I finally huffed in, red-faced and sticky. You'd think the humor of watching a fat kid jog would wear off.

But apparently, I was the joke that kept on giving.

So anyway, you can see why, when Agent Otter said, "Whoever crosses the finish line first" instead of "Whoever is fastest," I began to think. By the time my other classmates—all the SRS twelve-year-olds—lined up, that thinking had become planning. And by the time Agent Otter sounded the air horn, that planning had become . . . well. I don't want to use the word "scheming," but I'd understand if someone else did. But aren't spies—even spies in training—supposed to do a little scheming?

I was already sweating on account of the extended kickboxing session we'd just finished, in which I'd learned a variety of new ways to be pummeled. *Let it go,* I thought. *You're about to show them. You're about to win.* My classmates and I lined up, crouched down in near-unison. We were focused, determined. Otter snorted at us—which I guess was large-brutish-man language for *Ready?* We lifted our chins and stared at the hall ahead in response.

Another grunt. *Set?* We lifted our butts into the air. Then froze. No one moved, not a muscle, not a hair. *You can do this. You can do this.*

From the corner of my eye, I could still see Walter Quaddlebaum. As usual, he was wearing a T-shirt with the sleeves cut off to better display his admittedly impressive shoulder muscles. Even crouched, he was obviously the tallest guy in class. Less obvious, but still noticeable, was the idea of a beard growing around his chin. Who had a beard at twelve? Walter Quaddlebaum, that was who.

Last year he was skinny and short, and his hair stuck up in front like the crest on a fancy breed of chicken. Last year he failed the physical exam right along with me—a single exam that kept us from becoming junior agents. Last year he was also my best friend.

But things change, and today he was just another guy I needed to beat. And I had a plan all worked out for how I was going to do that.

The air horn sounded, ricocheting off the concrete walls. My classmates jolted forward; I was a second behind them, but only a second. We charged down the hall, sneakers squeaking furiously on the floor. The first stretch was a straightaway, a mad dash for the staircase. The other kids were, of course, faster, their ponytails and legs and impressive shoulder muscles steadily becoming farther and farther away. Walter hit the stairs first, taking three or four at a time. I was flying—well, for me, anyway—almost to the first step.

Mission: Win Agent Otter's Cruel and Unusual
Punishment Race
Step 1: Skip the stairs

I took a sharp right, away from the others. My lungs were beginning to burn. My toes were getting that awful tingly feeling, but I had to keep going. Alarmed agents lifted their eyebrows as I passed their open office doors. Ignoring them, I dived for the elevator at the end of the hall, jammed my fingers onto button 2, and punched Door Close.

The elevator played a smooth jazz song as it went up.

"Second floor," the female voice told me as I sprang out. I could hear my classmates again as they made the loop around the upper level. Something in my leg cramped, and I began to limp. Walter was still in the lead as he rounded the corner. His hair was flung in front of his eyes in a way that reminded me of the covers of Mom's romance paperbacks. My hair was in my eyes in a way that reminded me of a swamp monster.

I ducked into the break room and wedged my body behind a rolling cart of water jugs, bracing my legs against it. I pushed, hard. The wheels creaked, then inched forward. Walter streaked by the break room door. Jacob, Eleanor, and the others weren't far behind.

Step 2: Deploy obstacles

I took a deep breath and then pushed my feet as hard as I could. The cart shot forward, rolling out the door and into the hall, blocking the race route. Jonathan slammed against the cart, and jugs of water began to slide and whisk the other runners off their feet. *Yes!*

I staggered out into the hall, stumbling over a stray jug. Walter and the front of the pack—mostly kids who were already junior agents—were turning the corner ahead. I ran for the custodians' staircase in the opposite direction.

I knew where all the dry storage rooms, electrical closets, and staircases were at SRS. I'd like to tell you it's just because a great spy is keenly aware of his surroundings, but the truth is, I spent a lot of time avoiding my classmates by hiding in those places.

That time, however, was about to pay off.

Step 3: Use carefully researched alternate route

I flung open the door of the staircase, hurdled over a mop (okay, it was more of a stumble-almost-face-plant than a hurdle), and slid down the first few steps. Bursting through the first-level door, I cut across the hall through the Disguise Department.

"Hale! What do you think you're doing—Hey! Stop!" shrieked a woman meticulously painting a prosthetic nose. I grabbed on to her bookcase to help turn a corner; its display of wigs on Styrofoam heads crashed to the floor. Fake hair scattered everywhere. I kept going, plowing through the copy room, sliding on stray bits of printer paper. The production studio was ahead, filled with desks and props for making fake newscasts, anonymous clips, and the occasional staged wedding video for when senior agents needed to pose as a married couple. I heard footsteps pounding on carpet nearby—I was just in time.

Step 4: Everyone takes a trip

I crossed into the production room, grabbed a cable on the closest camera, then squeezed behind the green screen. I yanked the cable taut as the footsteps rounded the corner. *Crashes. Clatters.* Sophie, whom Walter had a crush on in second grade, used a word I knew her mother would have yelled at her for.

The green screen in front of me floated down across the scrambling bodies of my classmates. Was that all of them? It was impossible to tell from the limbs and loose shoes thrashing around under the fabric. I climbed over the pile of people (Sophie said a few more words that would get her in trouble) and took off.

There was no one ahead of me—the hall was blissfully empty. There was no sound other than my feet on the floor, thudding—slowly, I admit, but thudding along.

This must be what it's like to be the fastest. The strongest. The winner. I'd never really experienced the sensation before, so I tried to enjoy it and ignore the fact that my lungs felt like they were about to collapse.

I turned a corner—the dining hall doors came into view. This was amazing. I was going to win. I wasn't going to have to do pushups, which was still pretty fantastic, but that suddenly seemed a mere bonus to the *winning*. The dining hall looked strangely empty, mainly because my classmates weren't lounging in the tables by the doors, waiting to mock me. I would be there so early, *I* could lounge! I could . . .

Footsteps. Pounding fast behind me, way faster than mine. I didn't want to look, but I had to.

Walter.

His eyes were serious, his arms pumping furiously at his sides. He was gaining by the second. I begged my legs to move faster, and I think they tried, but they were no match for Walter's. He was a machine, flying past me. He was a dozen yards away from the doors, then ten, nine . . .

You might remember I said that once upon a time Walter and I were best friends. Which means once upon a time we told each other everything. Which means I knew exactly what would stop the machine that was Walter Quaddle-baum in his tracks.

I took a deep haggard breath. Puckered my lips, tilted my head back, and called out in a pitch-perfect impression of Walter's mother when she was angry:

"Waaaaaaaaaallllllllllllllyyyyyyyyyyyyyyyyyyyy!"

It really was pitch-perfect. I'd been around the Quaddlebaum family often enough to learn the tone, the length of the *y* sound, even the trill of the *a*. I'd also been around the Quaddlebaums often enough to say, without any reservation, that there was nothing, *nothing* an SRS spy could possibly face more terrifying than Teresa Quaddlebaum when she was angry.

Walter slammed his heels into the floor and whirled around. I could see his eyes darting back and forth across the hall, looking for his mother; his lips parted, probably to combination answer-apologize for whatever he'd done to warrant the tone.

I lumbered past him. I was only a few steps along when I felt Wally realize what had happened—one step, two steps behind me, he was building speed . . .

I flung myself forward, arms outstretched. My stomach slapped against the floor first, and I began to slide, slide forward, slide through the doors, into the dining hall. My shirt ruffed up, and my skin began to squeak against the tile as I drifted to a stop, inches away from the first row of tables.

I choked for the breath that had been knocked out of me, and I rocked onto my side, staring at the ceiling.

Was I dying? I certainly *felt* like I was dying, what with the way my heart was imploding and the beautiful glorious white light I saw above me. After a few desperate breaths, however, the glorious light became a plain old fluorescent one. Dizzy, blinking, I sat up.

Walter was in the doorway, staring at me. His expression was hard to name—was there a word for something between "amazed" and "horrified"? Agent Otter was beside him, silver whistle in his teeth, hands on his hips. *His* expression was easy to name: dumbfounded. He was dumbfounded, with his knees slightly bent, his eyes wide, his brows furrowed, like he had been about to whistle in the race winner, but someone hit Pause at the exact moment he saw it was me.

Wait.

It was me.

Step 5: Win

CHAPTER TWO

I wanted to whoop, to leap, to pump my fist into the air, but since I still felt a little like dying, I settled for grinning. The rest of my class stumbled down the hall, ponytails and shoes askew, looks of fury on their faces. It was hard to care—I had won, after all.

"You *cheated*," Walter snapped.

"What?" I said, but I was all wheezy so it came out: "Hhh-hhut?"

"He cheated!" Eleanor seconded, and Jacob folded his arms, nodding in agreement.

"He didn't run the whole route," Walter said.

"And he used a trip wire," Eleanor said.

"And I ran into a bunch of water jugs. I bet my trigger finger is broken," Sophie said, rubbing her hand for good measure. For the record her trigger finger looked just fine.

"And," Walter said, glowering at me (I swear, the guy never glowered when we were friends), "he distracted me at the end. You heard him, Agent Otter, right? He cheated."

I hauled myself to my feet with the help of a nearby table. I tugged my shirt down over my stomach, tried to slick the sweat off my forehead. The bubble of victory was still swelling in my chest, but I could feel how delicate it was becoming.

"I didn't cheat," I said, spitting the words out between pants. "Agent Otter said first one across the finish line wins. He didn't say we had to take the path."

"It was *implied*," Sophie said, and everyone—literally, every single one of my ten classmates—nodded in agreement.

"Quiet down, all of you," Agent Otter said gruffly, letting the whistle fall from his mouth. He pressed his tongue against his teeth, looked at the other students, who were clustered together like a pack, then at me. "That true, Hale? You cheated?"

"No!" I said, hitching up my pants and walking toward him. "I didn't cheat!"

"Then what would you call it?"

"I . . . I assessed the situation and strategized accordingly," I said, like I was reading an SRS textbook. Not that there's an SRS textbook, of course, but if there was, it'd say something like that.

"Sure, kid," Agent Otter said. "Pushups, everyone. Hale, my office, *now*."

I guess, in the end, I got out of doing pushups. So that was something.

It was little consolation, however, as I sat in Agent Otter's office. The room, much like Otter himself, was covered in hard surfaces and the color taupe. Taupe walls. Taupe desk. Taupe computer. Taupe flowers. I suppose the flowers had been yellow once, maybe pink, but they were dead and keeled over and had become crispy and, well . . . taupe. I'd probably keel over too, if I lived with Otter.

There was a quiet rap on the door.

"Ah," Otter said, glowering at me. "That'll be your parents now. Can't wait to tell them about *this* one. Come in!"

You know all those sayings? Ones like "The apple doesn't fall far from the tree!" and "What a chip off the ol' block!"? I can *promise* you they 're not true. Because I am slow and fat, and as graceful as a potato, and my parents . . . well.

My parents are known around here as "The Team." Not "a team"—"*The* Team." They were the first choice—sometimes the *only* choice—for highly dangerous missions. My mother speaks seven languages and had recently developed a new style of martial arts. My father is a master fencer and once hacked a terrorism ring's network using a calculator. They have so many awards and medals that turn up in weird places in our apartment—the linen closet, the pantry, dropped down behind the refrigerator . . .

The door clicked open and my parents walked in—I had my mom's dark hair and brown eyes, and my dad's broad shoulders, which looked manly on him but just made my waist look even wider. They both smiled briefly at me, and the sick feeling in my stomach subsided a little. Dad sat down on the left, Mom on my right; she put a hand on my arm gently, and even though it's a little embarrassing to be comforted by your mom when you're supposed to be becoming an elite spy, I was grateful for it.

"Mr. and Mrs. Jordan," Otter said, drumming his fingers on his desk.

"Please, Steve. There's no need for formalities," Mom said, all but rolling her eyes at Otter. They knew each other well because they'd all grown up together, just like Walter and I and the others. At SRS it was impossible to be a stranger—but that didn't mean it was easy to be friends.

Otter looked at me. His beady eyes would be charming on a gerbil but were terrifying on a full-grown man. "It seems we've had yet another incident with Hale."

"Oh?" Dad asked, unfazed. His hair was gelled and flawless, like mine in color, perhaps, but nothing else.

"Indeed. At the end of today's training session, he won a race by cheating," Otter said.

Mom frowned at me. "That doesn't sound like you, Hale."

"That's because it *isn't* like me," I said. "I didn't cheat."

"And now he's calling me a liar, I see!" Otter exclaimed.

Instead my Dad made his eyes steely and leaned toward Otter. I knew this position—it was the "getting answers" position. Hard stare, strong shoulders, firm jaw. That position could get everyone from my little sister to a criminal mastermind talking. Otter didn't stand a chance. He leaned back a bit in his taupe office chair and folded his hands together. He was trying to hide it, but I could tell he was nervous.

"Tell me what happened, Steve. Exactly what happened," Dad said coolly.

Otter stumbled through the story—he didn't know the details, really, so it wasn't much of a tale. Then my parents asked me to tell my side.

I went through the whole thing, lingering perhaps a little too long on the beauty of the green screen floating down on my classmates' heads.

They listened intently and then looked at each other. My parents did this thing—I guess it was a throwback from being partners long before they got married—where they had entire conversations without saying a word. I could tell they were having one now from the way their eyebrows lifted and fell, like their mouths were moving even though they weren't.

"Steve," Mom finally said aloud. "It sounds to me like Hale got the best of your trainees. I have to admit, I'm a little surprised. I mean, they couldn't jump over those water jugs? Couldn't see the trap in the production room? And Walter Quaddlebaum—my goodness. Didn't he just become a junior agent a few months ago? Yet he was thrown by the sound of his mother's voice? How embarrassing. For everyone."

"Walter's mother is the assistant director. It's not a bad thing for someone to stop when they hear her voice. But this isn't about my other students. It's about Hale. He knew the rules. Same rules they always have been—"

"Then you should have explained them the same way you always do," Dad said. "SRS agents are supposed to notice subtle variations in day-to-day behavior." Dad laughed and shook his head. "I don't know why I'm telling *you* that, Steve—of course you know! How foolish of me to forget the Acapulco incident."

I had no idea what the Acapulco incident was—I guessed something from back when Otter was a field agent? But the mention of it made Otter go totally silent and grit his teeth.

Dad continued to smile and then said, "Steve, I think it's important to remember that you, Katie here, Hale, and I—we all have the same goals. We're on the same team. Right?"

"Of course. But regardless," Otter said, his voice twisty, "I think it would be best if Hale saved his scheming for someplace else."

Ah. I knew someone would use the word "scheming."

Dad wanted to continue, I could tell, but Mom spoke first. "Of course, Steve. I'm sure he's learned a valuable lesson. Right, Hale?"

I looked at her, about to protest, but then sighed. "Sure have."

"Right. Well, I guess we're done here—" Dad began.

"Not quite. He still owes me fifty pushups," Otter interrupted as my parents and I rose.

"Not today, right, son?" Dad said, clapping me on the shoulder. "He won the race, after all."

And before Otter could argue, we swept out of the taupe office. The door drifted shut; we were only a few steps away when we heard an angry grunt come from inside.

Large-brutish-man language for "I hate Hale Jordan," if I had to guess.

CHAPTER THREE

Like everyone who worked at SRS headquarters—agents, secretaries, even the custodians—my family lived there as well, in our own apartment. This whole wing was full of families like our own—Walter and his mom were just a few doors down, actually. I'd never lived anywhere but apartment 300, and even though I was sometimes jealous of regular, non-spy kids who got backyards and swing sets, I have to admit, I couldn't picture anywhere else feeling like *home*.

We walked silently down the hall to our door. Dad unlocked it and stepped in first.

"Aha! Got you!" a tiny voice screeched.

I sighed, but Mom smiled. We stepped inside.

"Nice try, Kennedy," Dad told her, chuckling. "But I heard you snickering before I even took the keys out." Kennedy jumped down from her perch above the door, where I guess she'd balanced herself between the frame and the ceiling. Kennedy landed, forward-rolled, and sprang to standing like she expected applause.

"Did you really cheat and do an impression of Mrs. Quaddlebaum to beat Walter?" she asked me immediately.

"I didn't cheat!" I protested. "And how did you already hear about it?"

"Everyone knows about it. Including Mrs. Quaddlebaum," Kennedy said, tipping forward into a handstand. She followed me, walking on her hands. "You'd better watch it. You're seriously In the Weeds with her."

"Everyone's In the Weeds with Mrs. Quaddlebaum," I muttered, opening my bedroom door.

"Quiet, both of you. No one is In the Weeds with anyone. And neither of you is supposed to know that term," Dad called from the kitchen.

"Everyone knows about that too!" Kennedy shouted back, and it was true. It was code. An "In the Weeds" status meant the person was supposed to be eliminated on sight. I'd never seen a mission file that actually contained an In the Weeds target. These days, the only target SRS consistently eliminated on sight was my dignity.

"And if everyone jumped off a cliff, would you do that too?" Dad asked.

"That doesn't even make sense!" Kennedy said, groaning.

I used the distraction to step into my room. I shut the door just as Kennedy reached it.

"Hey!" she whined from the other side. "I wanted to show you a new cheer I learned!"

"You're not a cheerleader!"

"Yeah, and you're not Walter's mom, but you still pretended to be," she snapped.

"Kennedy, leave your brother alone!" Mom's voice boomed.

Kennedy sniffed, but then I heard her bound off, probably to scale some piece of furniture.

Kennedy wouldn't have any problem passing the physical exam when she tested for junior agent. I was actually surprised her teacher hadn't recommended she take the test already—she was only nine, but there wasn't an age minimum. Most people just didn't have the skill set to pass the exams before they were eleven or twelve. But Kennedy? She could pass it.

My little sister could be a junior agent before me. Great.

There were plenty of alternatives, of course—SRS had dozens of jobs for people who didn't become junior agents and then field agents. I could choose just about any specialty that didn't involve the physical exam, like becoming an agent in the Disguise Department, Tactical Support, or Research and Development. I could be a teacher, maybe, or an Explosives Analyst. I could easily pass the exam to get into Home Intelligence Technical Support—we called it HITS—which basically meant becoming one of the computer guys. Sit in the control room and shout at agents through a headset, then race office chairs, waiting to hack a security system or forge a clearance card or book a hotel room. They weren't bad guys, the HITS. We played video games in the control room when there wasn't an active mission, and unlike my classmates and the junior agents, they never once called me Hale the Whale, Haley's Comet, or Fail Hale.

But I didn't want to be in HITS. I wanted to be a field agent. I'd *always* wanted to be a field agent. They were in the thick of it—the danger, the excitement, the adventure. SRS teachers had a whole spiel about how "Everyone at SRS is important! Everyone has a role to play, from the teachers to the tech guys to the research crews!" but it never swayed me. I mean, field agents were the real heroes. Who wouldn't want to be a hero?

I stared at my ceiling for entirely too long, then rose and changed out of my training clothes. I could hear my parents clattering around, making fajitas—they always made fajitas when they'd had a "long day"—and any day where they had to talk with Otter usually qualified as long.

I opened my door and padded down the hallway.

"This is insane," my mother said, her voice unusually

rocky, even barely audible over the sound of food crackling on the stove. I froze, tilted my head, and listened like an antenna.

"We can't just do nothing, Katie," Dad said, voice grave. "Think about what it means."

"It doesn't matter," Mom said. "You don't just quit SRS."

I pressed against the wall, trying to creep closer. Who wanted to quit? Every now and then you'd hear a rumor about an agent wanting to retire and become a baker or something. But Mom was right—you couldn't just leave SRS. It sounds harsh, but we couldn't exactly have top-secret spies retiring to lives of pie making, you know? It was dangerous for everyone.

They argued in hushed voices for a moment, until I finally heard Dad hiss, "Project Groundcover is going to make SRS even more powerful!"

"I know, but if it goes wrong . . . We can't—not yet. Not until we've figured everything out. We have to play along, pretend like we don't know the truth . . ." Mom's voice dropped at the end and wavered like she might cry. Mom never cried! What were they . . .

"Hale!" Mom was suddenly in front of me, her eyes fiery and dark. I jumped down the hall, nearly tripping over the leg of my pants.

"I was just coming to dinner," I said quickly. "I didn't hear anything."

"Then how did you know there was anything to hear?"

"Okay, I heard *something*," I confessed. "About someone wanting to quit SRS? And something called Project—"

"Quiet." Dad looked grave now, way more serious than he usually was inside our apartment, and it scared me a little. "Forget everything you 'didn't hear,' okay, Hale? We shouldn't have been talking about work at dinnertime. We broke our own rule."

"You broke the rule?" Kennedy cried, crashing out of nowhere, an explosion of red hair and flailing arms. I really didn't understand how she could hear so well through all that hair. "Does that mean—"

"Yes, yes, yes," Mom said, waving a hand as she turned to go back into the kitchen. She seemed relieved to change the topic. Kennedy and I followed. "Darling? Hale caught us breaking our rule. Do we have any ice cream from last time?"

"Check the compartment?" Dad said. Mom ducked into the freezer, grabbed ahold of what looked like a frozen meatloaf but was actually a handle to a small but effective hidden compartment. A carton of vanilla-caramel-swirl ice cream was nestled snugly inside.

"I think there's enough for one more go-round," Mom said as she opened the carton to check. We probably didn't *really* have to hide the ice cream, even though it was technically considered contraband—SRS agents, after all, had to be in peak physical condition, so ice cream was a treat we got only when we were out on excursions. But Mom and Dad were The Team, so they got a little leeway. Besides, anyone who might turn us in could probably be bought off with a scoop.

"All right. After dinner. And then your mother and I start following our own rules about bringing work home, because you two have no idea how hard it is sneaking ice cream in here."

Mom handed me a stack of plates to set the table. Kennedy tried to slink away and avoid silverware duty, but Dad thrust a handful of forks at her before she made it out the door.

"Want to hear my cheer now, Hale?" Kennedy asked as she noisily dropped the last fork in its place.

"Sure."

"Okay!" she said, breaking out a wide grin. Kennedy slammed her hands against her sides and dropped her head. Taking a deep breath, she snapped her chin up and began to chant, slamming her arms at different angles around her body. It was a pretty stock cheer—lots of "Hey! Hey! Step back! We're on the attack!" type rhymes—but she did it with more enthusiasm in her little finger than I think I had in my entire body. When she finished, Kennedy leaped into the air and slid down into a perfect split, grinning and holding imaginary pom-poms aloft.

"What did you think?" she asked.

"I think . . . ," I began, pretending like I was going to

tease her. Her face fell; I smiled. "I think you're right. SRS really *should* have a cheerleading squad."

"I know," Kennedy said solemnly, rising. "But I'm going to convince Dr. Fishburn. You'll see."

I didn't think it was likely that Dr. Fishburn, SRS's director, was going to be convinced about anything that involved glitter and loud music, but I nodded. Kennedy had been obsessed with cheerleading for a year or two, ever since all the SRS kids had gone to the local high school's football game so we could see non-spy kids firsthand. We were supposed to study them so we could blend in better in case we became junior agents. Kennedy basically spent the entire time studying the cheerleaders (and so did a bunch of the boys in my class, but for a very different reason). I spent most of my time with Walter, taking notes and joking about how neither of us had a clue how football worked. I bet he knew how it worked now. Knowing about sports is probably something that just *happens* when you gain twenty pounds of muscle and lose one hundred and thirty pounds of Hale Jordan.

I took my seat at the table; Kennedy did some sort of crazy pommel horse move over the back of her chair to take hers. Mom and Dad joined us. We ate dinner fast, all eager to get to the ice cream, and as a result spent the next two hours sprawled out in the living room, clutching our over-filled stomachs. Dad quizzed Kennedy and me on SRS mission history, which devolved into him inventing stories and us adding on, Mom shaking her head at all three of us, smiling.

Here's the thing about SRS: it was a secret organization, and we were all in it together. We were all members of this great big impressive awesome thing. But sometimes? Sometimes, it was nice to be just a family—me, Kennedy, and Mom and Dad. A really little, probably sometimes a little boring, awesome thing. They felt like two entirely different places. There was SRS, where I had to prove myself, and there was apartment 300, where I could be just *Hale* and that was enough.

Or at least, it was enough until the next morning, when *everything* changed.

CHAPTER FOUR

"Hale, honey," Mom said the next morning, shaking a carton of orange juice harder than necessary before she poured a glass. "We've got a mission. Should be back late this evening. Emergency numbers for the neighbors and the medics are here." She tapped the refrigerator.

She paused to wiggle her torso, like something wasn't fitting right in her suit. It was some sort of stretchy combination of leather and Kevlar, with a zipper down the front and a turtleneck top. Mom tugged at her utility belt and then continued. "Try to get Kennedy to start her reading—I know, I know, but at least try—before dinner. We'll be back before you go to bed. Kennedy?" she shouted down the hall.

"I'm getting up!" Kennedy yelled, which was a lie.

"No cheers after six, got it? The people downstairs keep complaining."

"I'm getting up!" she yelled again. Kennedy didn't so much rise as she did melt out of bed, always leaving a trail of pillows and blankets behind her.

Dad laughed silently at Kennedy as he used the doorframe to stretch his shoulders. Mom finished her juice and joined him jogging in place for a moment. They moved to the living room to practice punching each other as I slogged through the rest of my oatmeal.

"Hale," Dad said, jumping backward and kicking at Mom's head. "It might be best if you stayed away from Agent Otter's bad side today, all right?"

"I try to stay away from all Agent Otter's sides. I'm not sure he'd like me any better even if I looked like the rest of the class," I grumbled as I rinsed my bowl out and set it in the sink.

"Hey now, Hale . . . ," Mom began sternly, ducking Dad's fist and kicking him hard in the back of the knee. He started to fall, but she swooped in at the last moment to push him back to his feet. She turned to me while Dad caught his breath. "Heroes don't always look like heroes." This was something she and Dad said a lot. They acted like it was just general advice, but I knew it was to try to make me feel better about myself.

"Villains don't always look like villains either," Dad

added. "Nothing is that simple. Just because Agent Otter isn't always very nice, doesn't mean he's your enemy. He's just still grumpy about being taken out of the field. Don't think he ever planned on being a teacher . . ."

"Yeah, but he got taken out of the field a billion years ago," I griped, but gave up when Dad shot me a pointed look. I changed the subject. "So, what's today's mission? Is it Project—" I fell silent, because I was about to say "Project Groundcover," but then remembered how serious Mom and Dad were about me never mentioning it again. They clearly realized what was about to come out of my mouth, though, because they froze and gave me matching stern looks.

"It's in Spain, I think," Mom said, without answering my question—which I suspected meant yes. She turned back to Dad. She bounced forward and back on the balls of her feet, waiting for him to strike.

"Spain?" Dad said, shaking out his arms. "I thought Fishburn said Seoul."

"Maybe. SRS has outposts in both places, don't they?" Mom shrugged. We lived in SRS's biggest location, but SRS was international—agents were tucked away throughout the world. It was sort of nice, knowing no matter where my parents went, they had allies nearby.

I leaned in the doorframe. "Do you really not know, or do you just not want to tell me?"

"Come on, Hale," Dad said, smiling. "Don't you trust us?"

"You're spies," I said warily, and turned to go to my bedroom and change.

"We're your parents!" Mom called back, laughing.

"Also spies!" I answered, shutting my door.

It was uniform day.

I often called uniform day by a variety of names—mostly involving words I heard Agent Otter muttering when the drink machine stole his dollar. I understand why spies have to wear black spandex—I do, really. You couldn't exactly crawl under a laser grid wearing shorts and a T-shirt. What I didn't understand was why anyone would *make* black spandex. Did a bunch of fabric company people get together somewhere to intentionally create the worst material on the planet? Or was it the result of some crazy factory accident? Surely, no one made this stuff on purpose.

"All right," Agent Otter said, walking briskly into our classroom. He scratched his head without looking at us. "Come on. Formation."

We hustled into neat rows in the center of the room, barely fitting in between the weight-lifting equipment. Otter turned to the door as the SRS uniform mistress entered.

Ms. Elma was an older lady with pale brown hair and a thin scar on one cheek. She was famous for this scar. She got it in a knife fight and sewed up the wound herself during her brief stint as a field agent. This was a story she liked to remind us of at every opportunity. "Your uniform doesn't fit? I'm so sorry. I suppose I'm not as good at sewing spandex as I am at sewing *my own face*." She was also known for her undying love for the Doctor Joe talk show. Let me explain Doctor Joe for you in one sentence: TV doctor with gray hair tells you to eat more salmon. I thought the show was super boring, but Ms. Elma—and a few of the other agents here—watched Doctor Joe like he was the soul mate they'd never met. I'd even heard that Ms. Elma wrote the guy love letters. Dad said she was just being a fan. Mom said she was just being delusional.

Tossed over Ms. Elma's right arm were dozens and dozens of SRS uniforms. Black spandex with blue trim that indicated our in-training status. "Stand up straight so I can see your shoulders," she barked, and we all jumped, straightening our spines. Ms. Elma chewed her tongue for a moment and then began to toss uniforms to us with complete confidence, despite the fact that she was hardly looking at them. "Go change, come back. *Fast*, please. And no primping, ladies. I don't have time for that. It's a uniform, not a prom dress."

One by one, students vanished from the formation as they ducked into the bathrooms to try on uniforms. All SRS trainees wore the hand-me-downs of older SRS members. Every now and then someone would get lucky and be fitted with a suit on its first go-round, but for the most part, our uniforms came complete with rips, tears, and burns, a bouquet of problems that we'd only add to before handing them down yet again. Once I got one that had a whole leg spray-painted pink.

I discovered that day that the only thing worse than black spandex is pink spandex.

"And . . . Hale Jordan," Ms. Elma said, a note of exhaustion in her voice. She looked down at the uniforms in her hand, then unfolded one and held it up in front of me. No. She tossed it over her shoulder and held up another, pursing her lips in a way that made her look like a duck. Finally she shoved the second uniform at me. "Try this, Jordan. It might work."

I nodded and trotted off toward the bathroom with my uniform. Walter and the other two boys in our class were still there, turning back and forth in front of the mirror, and I couldn't help but think Ms. Elma had warned the wrong people not to primp. Walter's arms were squeezed tightly into his sleeves; when I walked in, he turned to me and grinned.

"Hey there, cheater," he said. "Don't worry. My uniform doesn't fit either." With that, he hunched his shoulders forward and flexed his arm muscles until the seams of his already-battered uniform gave way along his biceps. He laughed, the sound all echoey in the bathroom, and high-fived Michael and Cameron, his junior-agent best friends.

They too had exceptionally large biceps, which I envied, and even larger foreheads, which was about the only thing I could silently make fun of them for.

"I wasn't worried," I answered. "*You* might be, though, when Ms. Elma sees your sleeves."

Walter's face paled a little, but he still managed to snort. "Yeah. Whatever, Whale."

Sometimes I pretended Walter hadn't changed due to puberty—that he'd just fallen into some toxic sludge—and that was why he transformed from totally-normal-guy Walter to worst-person-at-SRS Walter. One day, he's coming over after school; the next, he has a little facial hair and is busy in the afternoon. One day, he's huffing and puffing through the field exam along with me; the next, he's sprinting along with the junior agents, looking like a fairy godmother granted him the gift of calf muscles. It's not like Walter and I had a big fight or anything. One day we were friends, and the next, we weren't. Was it better or worse that way? I couldn't tell.

I walked into a stall, double-checked the door was locked, and began to change. My feet went in easily, as did my legs, but when it came time to pull the uniform over my torso, things came to a grinding halt. I shimmied and twisted and managed to get the shoulders up. I could even zip it a little, so long as I didn't need to do things like breathe or eat or have to pee. All in all, it was at least a better fit than my last uniform, which I couldn't even pull past my stomach. I walked out of the stall, trying not to move too much, and made my way back to the classroom.

"I don't know what happened, Ms. Elma. They just ripped!" Walter said as I reached the door. The Foreheads nodded earnestly behind him.

"Showing off," Ms. Elma snapped, and Walter shrank. I was pretty sure I saw his lip quiver. "Always with the showing off at this level." She said all this through a mouthful of pins, so everything sounded vaguely like a hiss. She was pinning the legs of a girl's uniform to mark for alterations—Ms. Elma was always talking about how our uniforms should feel like a "second skin." They should "fit like a glove." I questioned the sort of gloves Ms. Elma wore. I caught a glimpse of myself in the reflection of a chrome leg-press machine. I looked like I'd been eaten by an enormous seal.

"All right, Jordan," Otter said, motioning me toward Ms. Elma. "You're up."

Ms. Elma looked at me and shook her head. "What are we going to do about this?" I couldn't tell if she meant me or the uniform. "Perhaps we can use one of the others, sew some side panels in?"

Otter nodded. "Probably—"

"I wasn't talking to you, Steve," Ms. Elma said, waving him off without looking at him. Otter folded his arms, opened his mouth, but didn't say anything. Ms. Elma buzzed around me, tugging here, pushing there. She suddenly had a tape measure in her hands, though I couldn't have told you where it came from. "Right. Well, Hale, it'll take me a few days, but you'll have a uniform." She said this like the uniform was something I desperately wanted.

Twenty minutes later everyone who needed alterations had handed their uniforms back to Ms. Elma, who headed to the next classroom. Otter dug out a folder full of papers from a battered-looking leather satchel we all called a purse behind his back.

"Practice missions," he said. He rapped the folder against his palm, then sniffled in a way that made him look like a pug. Inside the folder were fake missions—many of which we'd been through before, and many of which were simulations of real, closed missions. He opened the folder and held out the papers, and my classmates dived, snatching and reading them hurriedly. Many were already running to the computer lab or the Disguise Department by the time I reached for one of my own.

Otter slammed the folder shut and withdrew it. I looked up at him and tried not to stare at his coffee-stained mustache.

"Jordan," Otter said in a sneery way. "I've got a special mission for you."

The first time I was sent on a "special mission" was when I was around Kennedy's age. Everyone else in my class was leaping off ropes onto sets of scaffolding. I, however, was swinging at the bottom of a rope like a human pendulum. When my teacher told me she had a special mission for me, one that involved leaving SRS, I was ecstatic. Everyone who wanted to leave SRS had to check out, of course, but kids that age never got to leave without supervision. Yet there I was, getting assigned a special mission! Going out on my own! The other nine-year-olds would be so jealous!

And then I realized the "mission" was really just a trip to get her some coffee at the shop outside headquarters.

It wasn't a mission. It was an errand.

I trudged toward the front office, trying to wash the bitter off my face—I didn't want Otter or anyone else to know how much stuff like this got to me.

"Oh, Hale, are you getting coffee?" the agent at the exit desk asked. She reached for her purse, and I began to wish I'd just snuck out through the loading docks.

"Nope," I said, and her face fell. "Dry cleaning for Agent Otter." The agent slouched in her chair and went back to staring at her computer screen. They didn't even bother having me sign out anymore, this happened so often.

I walked onto the elevator, bracing myself on the railing in the back—shooting up six flights in about a second always made me lose my balance. On the upper level the doors opened, revealing a grubby office building with vinyl chairs and orange-green tile. A young woman wearing lots of eye shadow—an SRS agent—looked up at me from a desk, tilted her chin to say hello, and then went back to painting her toenails fuchsia while the Doctor Joe show played loudly on her laptop. I breezed past her, out the doors, and onto the street.

SRS was located in a pretty little town called Castlebury, the sort of place where they strung Christmas lights between old brick buildings and had a parade for just about every holiday, right down to National Grapefruit Day. I'm serious.

Obviously, the people of Castlebury didn't have a clue that right under their feet was a program of elite spies and their spy-in-training kids. I glanced back at the building I'd just emerged from—a sign with missing letters read BR MBY COUNTY SUBSTITUTE MATHEMATICS TEACHER TRAINI G. The label pretty much meant no one would ever come inside. On the rare occasion someone did, the upper-level agent's job was to pretend to be an overworked reception- ist and ask the visitor about fixing copy machines until they left. No one on the outside knew about SRS—well, I guess some politician somewhere *had* to, since we were technically a government organization—but it just wasn't safe for everyone to know about us. A spy's greatest weapon was anonymity, after all.

It didn't take me long to retrieve the dry cleaning. I held the plastic garment bags over my head, but I still wasn't tall enough to keep the bottoms from dragging on the ground. The agent-slash-receptionist didn't even look up this time as I walked to the elevator and pushed the Down button.

The Down button didn't light up. I frowned and pushed it again. The light was probably just out. But no—I couldn't hear the sound of the elevator coming up. I turned to the receptionist, who was now looking at me with an eyebrow raised.

"Is it broken?" I asked.

"No . . . ," she said, frowning, and lifted the ancient cream-colored phone. "Hello? I've got that kid up here—the coffee kid, yeah. The elevator—*oh*."

The way she said "oh" was different. It was so different that I abandoned the elevator and walked toward her. She cupped her hand over her mouth, mumbled a few things into the phone, and then quickly hung up. She avoided my eyes. I saw her rubbing her toes together anxiously, ruining her wet nail polish.

Spies notice these things.

"Someone will be here in a minute to escort you back," she said. "The whole place just went on lockdown."

"Lockdown? Why?" Lockdown was serious—it meant something on a mission had gone wrong, so doors were locked, files were reviewed, and recordings were studied. No one came or went, so information couldn't be lost or shuffled or forgotten.

The receptionist's lips parted, but then we heard the

elevator begin to move. It chimed. The doors opened. My eyes widened—it was Agent Otter, and to his right was Dr. Fishburn, the director of SRS. He wore a shiny gray suit, the same color as his hair.

"Hale," Dr. Fishburn said. His voice sounded like that blue hand soap smells, all crisp and sharp and sinus clearing. "Come with us, please."

"What's going on?" I asked cautiously.

Otter spoke now, voice gruff and wildly unlike the snaky tone he normally took with me. "It's your parents, Hale. They've been compromised."

CHAPTER FIVE

Spies live dangerous lives.

I'd always known that—in fact, the danger was part of the reason I'd always wanted to be a field agent. But when I thought about my parents' job, I always saw being a spy mostly as dangling off buildings and karate chopping bad guys and stealing important hard drives—dangerous, sure, but also exciting and full of adrenaline and heroics. I never doubted for a moment that they'd be back, Mom retelling the nonconfidential parts of the tale and Dad struggling to shake his fake Russian accent. When your parents are The Team, you've got a whole houseful of medals proving that they can overcome any villain anytime and usually still make it home in time to start dinner.

But they weren't coming home. They weren't coming

home tonight or tomorrow, and probably not the next day either.

Because spies live dangerous lives.

"You understand, Hale," Fishburn said, putting a hand on my arm gently. Fishburn's office looked like him, all hard lines and metal surfaces and a half dozen locked file cabinets, one of which Otter was leaning against. "You understand that we don't think they've been—"

"Killed," I finished for him. I thought saying it aloud would make the whole idea of it easier to handle, but it didn't.

"Exactly. They're more valuable to The League alive," Fishburn said, nodding, like my basic comprehension impressed him.

I wasn't afraid of much. I'd gone through years of spy training, after all. Did I *like* getting beat up when my classmates and I sparred? No. But it meant I wasn't afraid of getting hit. I wasn't afraid of the dark, either—sure, I couldn't see spring-loaded rope traps in a blackout-training hall, but my classmates couldn't either. I wasn't afraid of heights, so long as I had decent climbing equipment, and I wasn't even afraid of getting caught while running a training mission, since being afraid of getting caught is the fastest way to actually getting caught.

I was afraid of The League.

They were a top-secret organization, just like SRS. The difference was, they were . . . well . . . evil. SRS was a secret, sure, but we were on the side of righteousness and morality and other good, legal stuff. The League, however, was a wholly criminal organization. You've heard of the mob? Of heist rings? Of the black market? All The League's work. Almost every major crime in the country traced back to them, and half the minor crimes did too. Two high-ranking agents like my parents would be invaluable to a bunch of criminals. They'd mine them for information, get it by any means . . .

My stomach twisted.

Fishburn continued, "I promise, we're doing everything we can to find them."

"Who are you sending out?" I asked. Agent Morgan? No, no, he was still nursing a broken leg from his last mission. Agent Green would be a decent second choice—though she didn't get along with the HITS, and that had botched more than one mission . . .

"We're working on it, Hale," Fishburn said, smiling. It was a fake smile, the sort we were taught to spot when we were seven. To be honest, I was a little insulted he thought I'd buy it.

"Who?" I asked again. "What's the plan? They've got to be at League headquarters. Are we sending a team in, or do we have someone inside?"

"Hale . . . ," Otter said, running his tongue over his teeth, like my name was stuck between them. He gave Fishburn a look that said, *Let me handle this.*

"Hale," Otter started again. "The mission your parents were on is Gold Level classified. *I* don't even know what it is. If we send in a team right now, we risk the mission."

I knew what it was—Project Groundcover, the mission that had had my parents so worried. I guess they'd been right to have been concerned. But how was some stupid mission, even a Gold Level classified one, more important than my parents? My hands were curled into fists so tight, my knuckles hurt. This wasn't *fair*. This wasn't *right*.

"We're doing everything we can, Hale," Fishburn said, stepping in. "Right now you need to trust us."

"I will as soon as you tell me what you're doing to save them." It was a bold thing to say, and I knew it. I stood up and walked out. Otter called my name, but I slammed the door anyway. I silently dared him to come after me.

He didn't.

Ms. Elma was at our apartment when Kennedy and I got back. She wandered around, too tall and lanky for the rooms, running her fingers across surfaces as if the whole place perplexed her. I knew I should actually be relieved to see her, because it meant SRS wasn't certain our parents were *never* coming back. Kids whose parents were gone for good—or who were away on long-term missions—lived in the dorm rooms on the upper floor. I'd never really thought of those kids as very different from me. We were all part of the SRS family, right? But now I realized just how different we were—and how badly I *didn't* want to be like them. I didn't want to live in a dorm room and not eat breakfast with my parents and not complain to my dad when Otter was being a jerk and never go to Mom when I needed to talk about Walter . . .

"I had the cafeteria send up dinner," Ms. Elma said in a voice I think was supposed to be warm, but was still so cold, it froze my thoughts. She motioned toward the kitchen table, where she'd placed Styrofoam takeout boxes at three of the four seats. She flicked the overhead light on, which we never used because it made a buzzing sound Mom hated, and poured us glasses of water with too much ice.

Kennedy, who had barely let go of my hand since we'd met up outside Fishburn's office, looked up at me, then exhaled and pulled me over to the table. She took her normal seat silently, and I took mine.

Ms. Elma started to lower herself into a third chair.

"That's Dad's seat," Kennedy said crossly.

Ms. Elma raised her eyebrows. "Is there somewhere else I should sit then?"

I had to give her some credit—she seemed to be *trying*. But trying to step in for our parents was sort of like me trying to do a pull-up. It just wasn't going to happen.

Kennedy didn't respond but kept her eyes hard on Ms. Elma. Even her freckles seemed to be glaring.

"Right," Ms. Elma said tersely. "What if I go watch television while I eat then? Give you two a little . . . sibling time."

She rose, breathed slowly, and settled in the other room. I heard the sound of her opening and rifling around in her takeout box. Kennedy and I stared at our own Styrofoam boxes like they might contain explosives.

"Wait . . . is there no television here?" Ms. Elma called from the other room.

"No," I answered. "We're not allowed."

"Not even a little one? What do you do at night?"

"We play board games! Mom and Dad don't like television!" Kennedy snapped, and I could see tears welling up in her eyes. I rose, nearly knocking my chair back, and went around the table. Kennedy hugged me so hard, her fingers almost touched and I thought she might break my ribs. Freeing myself, I knelt down. I shook my head at her.

"Don't cry," I said as Kennedy's face twisted up. She squeezed her eyes shut as hard as she could and fell forward, dropping her head to my shoulder.

Kennedy whisper-sniffed. "Everyone's saying Fishburn is just giving up on them."

"That's ridiculous," I said. "He just doesn't want to risk the mission."

"No one's doing anything!" she protested, sitting back. Her eyes were wide, her skin pale under the overhead light.

I exhaled. "How about we go to bed? It's later than it feels."

"It's barely seven," she said, wiping her nose with her hand. Still, we left our takeout containers untouched and went to brush our teeth. I helped Kennedy into her bed and pulled up the covers, then found Tinsel, the stuffed hedgehog that she liked to pretend she didn't need anymore, but definitely did at times like this.

"Are you going to tell me a story?" she asked, her voice meek. Dad used to tell us bedtime stories about when he was a new agent—the time he mixed up German for Icelandic, or when he used three sticks of chewing gum to hotwire a car. I knew Dad didn't tell her stories every night anymore, but I sat down on the edge of her bed anyway.

"I don't have any good stories," I said. "I'm not an agent."

"You could tell me about winning the race yesterday," she suggested, picking at Tinsel's quills. "I mean, your version."

"The *true* version, you mean," I said, and launched into the story. I started quietly with just the details, but as I went on, things got bigger and louder, until I was crashing across the room in a re-creation of the way I slid into the cafeteria ahead of Walter. Kennedy was giggling, her thin lips pulled into a broad smile. When I left the room, she was still awake, staring at the ceiling, and I knew she would cry again before she fell asleep. But truthfully? So would I.

I ran into Ms. Elma in the hall—literally ran into her, hard enough that she bounced back a few steps.

"You didn't eat your dinner," she said politely. "You're supposed to eat it."

"We aren't hungry," I answered, wondering if Ms. Elma

was really the best person to be put in charge of me and Kennedy. Surely, she'd do better with something less human and more, say, houseplant?

"Oh. I'll save it then. You'll probably be hungry later. I finished alterations on your uniform." She held out a limp pile of black spandex and gave me an almost warm look, as if the fast turnaround was something to be appreciated and admired. She cleared her throat. "I know, Jordan—*Hale*—that you want someone to charge in and save them. We all wish it were that easy. But SRS agents can't just sneak into League headquarters. It's risky for everyone—including your parents. And the mission. You've got to think of the mission."

"Right."

Ms. Elma nodded, twisting her lips in a way that made her face look like it contained too many bones. Finally she patted me on the shoulder and retreated back to the living room. I went to my bedroom and shut the door. I wanted to lock it, but I was worried Kennedy might want to come in sometime during the night. I changed into pajamas and climbed into bed, staring at the glow-in-the-dark stars that covered my ceiling.

The truth was, everything Ms. Elma and Dr. Fishburn had said made sense. With my parents gone, SRS couldn't just throw more agents out into the world and hope for the best. Agents were precious resources, the product of years of training and preparation. And a mission—even a mission I didn't really know anything about—was always the priority.

But I wasn't an agent.

I then began to undeniably, unabashedly *scheme*.

CHAPTER SIX

It was almost seven o'clock in the morning, and I could see a line of light under my bedroom door. Judging from the clattering and hissing, I gathered Ms. Elma was futzing around with Dad's espresso machine. I exhaled, steeled myself, and then crept out of my bed slowly so my mattress didn't creak. I ran in place as quickly—and quietly—as I could, till my lungs began to ache. I then leaped back into bed, yanked my blankets up, and felt at my cheeks—flushed and damp.

Perfect. Go time.

"Ms. Elma?" I called out weakly, my voice barely a whisper. I waited. Another hissing sound. I was pretty sure she'd just broken the milk steamer.

"Ms. Elma!" I called again, louder this time. I heard a sigh and the sound of a coffee cup being put down too hard, and a few minutes later Ms. Elma swung my door open. I curled into the smallest ball possible and coughed. "I don't feel good."

Ms. Elma's eyes widened. "You're bleeding? Broken bone? I'll call medical—"

"What? No. I'm just *sick*."

Ms. Elma didn't look like she fully understood what I meant.

"I just feel sick. You know. Headache? Like I might throw up?" I said. Ms. Elma blinked. I suspected Ms. Elma had never called in sick. "I think I just need to get some rest," I finished.

Ms. Elma rocked back on her heels warily. "Well. All right. Do you want some . . . medicine?"

I shook my head.

"Do you want some . . . soup?"

I shook my head again.

"Are you sure I shouldn't call medical?" Ms. Elma asked again, almost desperately.

"No, no, I'll pull through," I said, firming my lips like I was being very brave about my sudden illness. "I'll probably just sleep most of the day. Don't feel like you have to stay here—I know you probably planned on going home for a few hours."

"Mmmm," Ms. Elma said, grimacing in a way that made clear she had not only planned on going home but badly wanted to. "I'll just stay here."

"Really?" I mumbled, letting my words drift off like I could barely stay awake. I yawned enormously; through my half-closed eyes I saw Ms. Elma wrinkle her nose at my open mouth. "That's so nice of you. I can't believe you're going to miss Doctor Joe's Present-Palooza."

"Present-Palooza?" Ms. Elma asked, her overplucked eyebrows shooting up so high, they pulled at her scar.

"I heard the receptionist talking about it while I was out getting Otter's—*Agent* Otter's—dry cleaning," I said. I reached over and knocked around a set of binoculars as I fumbled for the tissue box on my nightstand. I feebly tugged one from the box, then used it to mop at my forehead, waiting till Ms. Elma leaned forward eagerly to continue. "He's giving away all sorts of stuff to people in the audience, and is sending some sort of wrinkle cream to anyone who calls in every time he says 'carrot top.' You know, maybe it's tomorrow though. I don't really remember . . ." I coughed and hugged my blankets closer. The flush from my face was beginning to fade . . .

Ms. Elma nodded. She ran her tongue over her teeth as she left the room.

A half hour later there was yelling, crying, and things breaking. Ms. Elma was trying to get Kennedy ready for school and didn't know my parents' tricks; with five minutes to go before class started, Kennedy was still shouting about not being able to find her uniform shoes. ("They're covered in stickers of pink owls. Yes, pink owls! *Who cares?*

They're my shoes!") Ms. Elma responded by muttering under her breath about how in her day, back when she'd gotten the scar on her face, agents didn't always get shoes. I didn't believe her, and I suspected Kennedy didn't either. Finally the supernova that was my little sister found her shoes and went to class. It was nine o'clock. The Doctor Joe show came on at ten . . . Nothing to do but wait.

"Hale?" Ms. Elma said through my closed door at nine fifty-five. I grinned beneath my blankets.

"Mmmm?" I answered groggily.

"I'm going to run downstairs for a few minutes. If anyone asks, I'm just getting some . . . personal effects. I'll be back, all right?"

"Mmmm," I answered.

She left in such a hurry that I wasn't sure, at first, if she'd left at all—the door didn't click all the way shut. Finally, when I was sure she was gone, I tossed my covers back. I rose and pulled my uniform on—I hated it, but I might need it—and some street clothes on top of it. Then I ran into Kennedy's bedroom.

Walking into Kennedy's room was sort of like being punched in the face with a pack of highlighters. The walls were covered in neon pink and purple posters, most depicting animals, cheerleaders, or animals being cheerleaders. Her floor was a disaster of books and candy-colored stuffed toys, along with a few dolls with catlike eyes and plastic, glitter-filled jewelry. I grabbed a stuffed turtle with a peace sign on its back and a variety of bears and cats, several of which were tie-dye. I nearly tripped over a set of lime green pom-poms on the way out of the room.

Back in my bedroom I shoved the toys beneath my blankets until they were feasibly shaped like me sleeping. It was an old trick, but it would have to do—there was no time to rig a voice-activated response system, which was a shame, since I aced that class last year. In the kitchen I left a bowl filled with a few drops of milk and a half handful of cereal, so it looked like I'd emerged to eat something. I left the milk out for good measure and then glanced at the clock.

I had plenty of time—despite the lack of Present-Palooza, I suspected Ms. Elma wouldn't be able to turn off Doctor Joe—he was her long-lost soul mate, after all. Still, the sooner I left, the better. I finished the pretend breakfast scene by pulling a chair out from the table and then I went down the hall to my parents' bedroom. I lifted a hand to knock before remembering I didn't have to—they weren't inside—then turned the knob and opened the door.

I froze as cool air swept across my face, air that smelled like Dad's deodorant and Mom's face cream. Their bed was made, the closet door was shut, and my mom's wedding rings sat on the nightstand—she never wore them out on missions, but she always put them back on first thing when she came home. I could still see their footprints in the carpet. I closed my eyes.

The mission. Think about the mission.

Not their mission—*my* mission. I had to focus. I gritted my teeth, opened my eyes, and hurried across the room. I flung open the closet door. Mom's clothes were on the right, Dad's on the left; I grabbed an armful of dress pants off their hangers, which swung wildly, knocking against the wall. I shoved the pants into a mesh laundry bag and slung it over my shoulder, then took a handful of Dad's loose change off his dresser.

With everyone at work or in training, it was easy to make it down the hall relatively unseen. I knew cameras were on, but I also knew the sight of me lugging around a bag of laundry wasn't exactly something that put the HITS on high alert. I forced myself to look unrushed on the way to the front desk.

"Morning, Hale," the agent at the front desk said sweetly as I walked in. "I heard about The Team. Don't worry. I'm sure Dr. Fishburn has a plan."

"Me too," I said, which, if you ask me, was one of my most convincing lies to date. I nodded toward the laundry bag on my shoulder. "Dropping off dry cleaning."

"Agent Otter has *more* dry cleaning?" the exit desk agent said, shaking her head at the bag. "Something's wrong with that man."

"No kidding," I said, smiling at her. The agent didn't see it—she had already gone back to filling out spreadsheets. I stepped around her desk and walked to the elevator. I waited till the doors closed, then let out a deep breath. I don't know why I was relieved—breaking out of SRS was the easy part.

It was breaking into The League that was going to be difficult.

CHAPTER SEVEN

Castlebury had a single train line that went straight into the city—it was impossible to go wrong. I climbed on, the bag of laundry wedged between my legs, and I tried to relax as we rumbled along. We stopped a dozen or so times on the way, picking up an ever-stranger assortment of passengers. By the time the city appeared ahead—gray lines that became buildings that became windows and bridges and cars—we'd collected a few hippies, a few students, and what sounded like seventeen crying babies, whose screams seemed to make my hidden SRS uniform fit even tighter. I began to wish I'd stolen one of the SRS's helicopters instead. I'd flown one in simulations—how different could a real one be?

Where Castlebury was old bricks and potted plants, Fairview was steel beams and parking meters. People didn't notice me here any more than they did in Castlebury, but the difference was, in the city they seemed to be *intentionally* not noticing me. Which was just as well, really—I didn't want to be seen. I knew the city well enough, since I'd visited it on outings with my parents and the occasional class trip, but being here alone felt very . . . scary? No. Not scary. It felt *big*. Like the whole place could swallow me, and it made me grin and sort of shake all at the same time. I cut around delis, past food trucks cooking mysterious meat products, and away from the larger buildings.

Toward The League's headquarters.

I knew exactly where League headquarters were. Everyone at SRS did—and everyone at The League, I reasoned, probably knew where we were. I mean, if there were grizzly bear dens near your house, you'd know where they were, right? I took a right at a grocery store and walked past a group of Campfire Scouts wearing khaki-colored sashes and hawking cookies to every passerby.

And then . . . there it was.

Like the SRS, The League occupied a relatively nondescript building, though theirs was big, made of metal and glass and stretching toward the sky. I suspected the height was more of a distraction—most of their facilities were surely underground, safely buried beneath the city. The letters EBP were on the side of the building in bright red block characters, but I was pretty certain they didn't stand for anything—they were just the sort of letters that a regular person would nod at, assuming they belonged to some rich corporation. The building had wide stairs leading up to it, where people stopped to talk, eat lunch, or stare at the pigeons that hung out around a weird twisty statue.

This was where my plan ended. I'd never gotten close enough to The League's building to really study it before, so I couldn't plot how to break in till this exact moment. I pretended to be bored as I analyzed potential points of entry—my teacher from last year would be proud, I bet, since she did two months of classes on breaking into secure buildings.

The League had cameras by the front doors. Probably more inside. There were likely vents or windows on the lower levels, but slipping through those was for people six sizes smaller than I was. The roof was out, since I didn't have air support, as was burrowing underground. Basically, the only way into The League, for me, was through the front doors. Which meant I needed a way in—one that would not only get me through the front doors, but past the agents on the other side.

I rose and walked away from the building. I ducked into the grocery store and dared to spend a handful of quarters in the vending machines across from the bathroom doors—because I'd skipped breakfast, I was too hungry to think straight. The honey bun I bought was dry and mealy, but it was something. I shoved the laundry bag into the corner of the largest stall and leaned against the door as I ate.

Think. And think fast, because your parents are in that building, and you're all they have.

Except I had nothing at all. I closed my eyes and commanded myself to think. *Focus on the mission, Hale. Come on . . .*

Wait. I didn't have nothing. I had two dollars in change and a bag of laundry.

Which meant I had a plan.

Mission: Break into The League
Step 1: Acquire necessities—knife, tape,
and cookies

The knife and tape were easy—I wandered the aisles of the grocery store until I found a guy shelving cans of tuna fish. He seemed like a nice enough guy, really. So I felt bad about intentionally shattering one of those four-gallon glass jars of pickles one aisle over. I shuffled away quickly; the tuna stocker ran past me and groaned. Muttering something about floor wax, he stomped off to get a broom.

Meanwhile, I snuck back to the tuna fish, snatched his box cutter, and shoved it into my pocket.

Knife? Check.

Next I grabbed a bunch of the stickers from the bulk food section. They were supposed to seal the bags of self-serve grains.

Tape? Check.

Cookies were slightly trickier. I considered just stealing them, but I already felt pretty high profile after arriving with a laundry bag and breaking a pickle jar. I couldn't afford to get thrown out, or worse: reported to the police.

Instead I made my way to the bakery section. A glass case housed two dozen types of cupcakes and pies and éclairs and all sorts of desserts the SRS would never let us touch, much less eat. The woman behind the bakery counter smiled at me with overly glossed lips.

"Are these samples?" I asked her. A plastic plateful of tiny sugar cookies with sprinkles sat on top of the case.

She nodded, then smiled. "Help yourself!"

Her smile faded as I grabbed one of the nearby bakery boxes and shoveled almost the entire tray of cookies inside. I shrugged. She *had* told me to "help myself."

Cookies? Check.

I yanked an OUT OF ORDER sign off one of the drink machines across the hall, and then I stuck it against the bathroom door to give myself a little privacy.

Step 2: Put together the perfect disguise

I dumped the laundry bag out on the floor and reached for a pair of Dad's khakis. I studied them for a moment and then folded them in half so the cuffs of the legs met each other. I pulled out the tuna guy's box cutter. Carefully, I drew the blade through the pants, right below the pockets.

It took a few cuts before I finally broke through the layers of fabric. Then I grabbed the bulk foods stickers and looped them so they were sticky on both sides. Folding the ends of the pant legs over, I ran the stickers along the edge, until they were flat and smooth, as clean a line as if the fabric had been sewn that way.

All right, the moment of truth. I ducked between the two pant legs, letting one end rest on my left shoulder and the other on my right hip so it became a khaki-colored sash. I picked up the box of cookies and looked at myself in the mirror.

Deep breaths, Hale.

Half of being a spy is lying. What most people don't realize—and what SRS students learn in year one—is most of that means lying to yourself. It's easy to trick a stranger into believing a story. After all, they don't know you—why shouldn't they believe you? But fooling yourself is something else entirely because you have to bury the real you so far beneath the lie that it doesn't have a prayer of poking its head up. Once you've fooled yourself, though, that's when your cover is perfect.

So, even though I'd never been a Campfire Scout, even though I'd never even been camping, period, I walked toward The League with total confidence. After all, I was a Campfire Scout—I had the sash and cookies to prove it. This was the EBP office building, nothing more. I was just there to hand out cookie samples. What did I have to worry about?

Step 3: Walk through the front door

I reached forward, pushing through the revolving glass door . . .

I froze. The lobby ceiling soared all the way to the top of the building, with plants hanging off the elevator landings on each floor. Everything was marble, but the building wasn't quite as sleek as SRS's—it smelled more like oranges and leather shoes than cleaner. Behind a broad wooden desk with a bowl of mints in the corner was a skinny man wearing a vest and a dotted tie; other than him, the lobby was totally empty. He gave me a confused look.

"Can I help you?" he asked.

"Yes, sir," I said, grinning like the cheerleading animals plastered around Kennedy's bedroom—like this moment was the best moment, ever, ever, ever. I hustled over to him, dimming the smile when he seemed more concerned than charmed.

"I'm Walter Quaddlebaum from Campfire Scouts Troop three seventy-one, sir, and I'm here to offer samples of our new line of Campfire Scout cookies. Would you be interested in trying one?" I said all this exactly, like I was reciting it from a script a troop leader gave me.

"Oh!" The man's eyes lit up. "Oh, I shouldn't. I shouldn't . . . Sugar and all . . ."

He looked from side to side, like someone might pounce

on him if he said yes, then grinned at me and reached for a cookie.

"Thanks," I said cheerily. "I'm supposed to give out the box to earn my Bakemaster Badge."

"Of course! If you leave them here, I promise I'll—"

"Oh, no—I have to give them out myself to get the badge."

The receptionist looked at me and blinked. "But can't you just tell your scout leader you gave them away yourself?"

I widened my eyes.

"You . . . you want me to lie?" I said this at nearly a whisper, like I'd never heard anything so horrific.

The receptionist hurriedly shook his head and held up his hands. "No, of course not, but I can't let—"

"I don't have *any* badges yet," I said, lifting my pants-sash woefully. "And you want me to lie to get my first one?"

I sniffed and tensed my face until a few tears dropped from my eyes. My face always turned neon red when I cried, which usually was embarrassing—and part of the reason I never, ever let Walter and his minions make me cry—but right now that fearful color was coming in handy, along with the fact that I looked about as nonthreatening as a kitten. I mean, a crying kid bearing cookies? I let my lower lip quiver, just to complete the act.

"Don't, don't, don't cry," the receptionist begged. "I don't want you to lie, of course not."

He frowned and glanced down the hall directly behind

him. "How about you go down that hall, then curve around and come back up here? It shouldn't take long. Drop it in any of the open office doors."

"What about the closed ones? Should I knock?"

"Oh, no one works in those—we're pretty short staffed these days," the receptionist said, looking back down the hall warily. "All right, go on."

I grinned, wiped my tears away with the back of my hand, and scurried down the hall. Glancing over my shoulder, I saw him look down at his watch—I had ten minutes, probably, before he'd become suspicious and come after me.

I could work with ten minutes.

Step 4: Find Mom and Dad

CHAPTER EIGHT

Let me explain something about SRS.

We had offices. Plenty of them—halls of them, in fact. But agents were normally using them to practice kickboxing or hack into a computer's mainframe or learn to speak Portuguese. Sure, there were the few odd people who sat quietly on computers all day gathering intel, but they were definitely in the minority, and they still looked impressive, typing away, then pausing to scribble down notes. I guess I expected to see something similar at The League.

Instead I saw . . . office people.

People lining up pencils on their desks. One guy playing golf, hitting a ball into a coffee cup. Another pretending to work busily, but actually looking at small, hairless dogs on a dodgy animal-rescue website. Everyone happily took cookies, and no one seemed terribly concerned about my presence. Was this a trap? It had to be a trap—this was *The League*, after all.

I came to the corner where I was supposed to take a right and emerge back in the lobby. I glanced in an office and looked at a clock—I'd been gone for four minutes.

That meant I had six more minutes to get as deep into The League as I could. Which meant it was time to go beyond the open doors. Time to go beyond this single floor. There was a heavy metal door to my left, totally unlike the wooden office doors. I pushed it open—a stairwell. I leaned my head over the stair rail and took stock. I was about only five levels from the very bottom, which seemed the most practical place to hold prisoners. I took note of an emergency exit door, just in case I needed one later, then hurried down the steps.

Five flights of stairs later, my shins were burning. I stopped at the basement level; ahead of me was a long, musty-smelling hallway. Every door was labeled: WATER, ELECTRICAL, CUSTODIAN. Maybe they were mislabeled to throw intruders off.

I opened the custodian's closet. Brooms.

Electrical door. Fuse boxes.

Water. Water softeners.

At the end of the hall was a larger set of doors, not entirely different from the cafeteria doors back at SRS. It wasn't until I got a little closer that I could read the label—TRAINING AND CONDITIONING. I supposed it was as good a door as any other I'd seen, so I pushed it open and walked into the room.

The gym back at SRS was full of sleek equipment. Chrome weight machines, black punching bags, treadmills, stationary bikes, and those weird stair-step machines that no one ever wanted to use. Otter always told us it was a room dedicated to our "personal best," which maybe was true for some people. For me it was more of an ode to my misery. Everything there smelled like lemon cleaner, burning rubber, and sweat, though not always in that order.

The League gym was very, very different.

For starters, it smelled like old foam, spilled soda, and grease—in that order. The walls were painted a sort of creamy white, like the color of the good vanilla ice cream, and there were little bits of tape all over them from where posters or signs had been stuck up at some point. There were jump ropes hung haphazardly on hooks, some white and mauve weight machines in the far corner, and a rubber track that ran around the exterior of the whole thing.

There were also two people staring at me.

I remained calm.

That was what I'd been trained to do, after all, the thing that teacher after teacher had beat into my head as step one in any risky situation: remain calm.

Step two: assess the situation.

The people staring at me were kids—my age, probably, maybe a tiny bit younger. The boy was short with knobby joints and hair that stuck up like someone had just rubbed it with a balloon. He was arranging odds and ends from the gym—a three-pound weight here, an uninflated bike tube there, a few yoga balls at the end—into some sort of elaborate pattern, almost like a maze. The girl beside him had his black hair, but hers was neatly pulled into two short French braids. She also had glasses, the big kind that looked like they should belong to a history professor, and she was holding something that looked like several cell phones duct-taped together.

I dropped the box of cookies to the ground and braced myself. Hands to my face, fists ready—I could maybe take one of them out, but two? They had to be partners, if they were in here training together, which meant they knew exactly how to take out a target together. The girl looked particularly scrappy. I was never good with scrappy.

"Five-second rule!"

I frowned. It was the boy who yelled it—no, *screeched* it, really. He dived forward. I hunched down, prepared to fling myself on top of him and hold him down—I mean, hey, I've got extra body weight, I might as well use it, right? I took a step forward, ready to land on his legs . . .

He grabbed a cookie and crammed it into his mouth,

looking pleased with himself. The girl behind him crinkled her nose, making her big glasses rock on her face.

"You know that five-second rule thing isn't true, don't you?" I asked.

"Says the person who isn't getting any cookies," the boy answered, his words muffled as bits of sugar cookie fell from his mouth. I realized his shirt had a picture of a robot fighting a dinosaur on it.

I did not know how to assess this situation. The boy stooped for another cookie.

"Ben . . . ," the girl said. "They're his."

"He dropped them!"

"That doesn't mean—"

"Who are you?" I asked. I meant for the words to be sharp, hard—more of a demand than a question, but I sounded more confused than anything.

The girl stepped forward. Her eyelashes were so long, they brushed against her glasses, and she had little heart-shaped stud earrings in. We weren't allowed earrings at SRS—no tattoos, piercings, or anything that would make it easier for an enemy agent to identify us. The girl must have realized I was staring, because she reached up and touched one of the earrings absently, and then shrugged.

"I'm Beatrix," she said. "He's my brother, Ben. Our uncle's an analyst. Do your parents work here?"

"My . . . uh . . . they . . ." *Quick—think, Hale, think.* These two weren't agents—or if they were, they had *incredibly* good cover characters. I stood a better chance with the cover characters than in a fistfight, though, so I decided to play along. "They work in intake."

"Intake?" Beatrix asked, squinting at me.

"Prisoner transport," I clarified. "My dad. He just started the other day."

"Huh," Ben said. "Weird. Uncle Stan didn't say anything about hiring new people. That's sort of a big deal." I waited, expecting him to press me further, ask questions I didn't have the answers to. Instead he shrugged and said, "So why are you dressed like a Campfire Scout?"

"Because I am a Campfire Scout."

"You don't have any badges."

"I just joined." I cursed myself for not spending more time coming up with a cover character of my own. I aced the class in false identities earlier this year, and there I was, totally bombing at it in the field.

"Want to see my machine?" Ben asked brightly.

"What?"

"My machine. I call it the RiverBENd," Ben said, motioning to the deliberately ordered collection of gym things. "It pours me a glass of water."

I looked at the row of things—there was a broken trampoline and a janitor's water bucket among the chaos—and frowned. With a grin, Ben dashed over to one end, where a yoga mat lay curled up atop a rolling cart. He slowly, carefully placed a finger on the mat, then nudged the mat forward.

The mat unfurled. When it flipped down, the edge caught the end of the bicycle tube. The tube snapped forward, sending three hand weights rolling down a ramp made of towels stretched tautly. The final weight flipped off the end, triggering a seesaw that bounced a yoga ball up into the air. The ball, in turn, slapped the end of a jump rope, which swung forward then back, spiraling itself around a mop. The mop tilted to the front of its cleaning bucket, upsetting a broom. To my amazement—shock, wonder, delight, even—the broom handle fell forward, striking the button on the water fountain.

The fountain turned on and an arc of water shot up into the sky, missing the drain by a mile. It cascaded beautifully down toward a plastic cup on the ground. I held my breath as . . .

It missed. By an inch, give or take. We all exhaled in disappointment.

"Oh, come on!" Ben yelled in frustration, turning around and kicking a basketball so hard, it bounced back off the wall and whizzed by my head.

"I told you," Beatrix said. "I told you the pressure was wrong. You tested it when you were pushing down on the water fountain thing, but the broom doesn't push as hard as you."

To prove her point, she turned the cell phone contraption around so that we could see the screen. On it was a fancy drawing of the arc of the water fountain, an X where the cup should have been placed.

"Trust the Right Hand," she finished sagely.

"The what?" I asked, worrying this was a code name for a weapon.

"The *Right Hand*. My phone? 'Cause it's always in my hand? Get it? It's a joke."

I tried to laugh, but it came out as sort of a weird *huck-huck* noise.

"Okay, hang on. I can fix it," Ben muttered, and walked to the water fountain. He repositioned the cup, and then began to meticulously backtrack through the machine, putting all the parts in their original positions. Beatrix helped him rebalance the weights.

"So . . . um . . . anyway," I said. "So, my dad works in prisoner transport, and I was supposed to check in with him after I gave away the rest of those cookies . . ." I glanced at the floor. *Lie, Hale, remember how to lie.* "I can't think of where it is, though."

"We don't have anything like that," Ben said, shrugging. "I think we used to? Maybe? Maybe we could ask the receptionist?"

"Oh, I don't want to bother him," I said. "Maybe you call it something different, something I'm not used to. Holding?"

Beatrix shrugged, and Ben just returned to lining up the yoga balls.

They knew. They *had* to know, and the fact that they weren't telling me made me more convinced than ever that they were agents undercover. It also convinced me more and more that they were stalling. We were in a race of wits, and I needed to stay ahead. The only way to do that would be by beating them to a confession.

I firmed my jaw, stood up straight, and tried to make my eyes all coal-like, same as on Dad's "getting answers" face. I reached down and tugged at my shirt, stretching the neck down far enough that my uniform—and the SRS logo on it—was revealed. Telling the truth was definitely *not* something I learned in training, but desperate times called for desperate measures, right?

"Enough," I said coolly. "No more charades. Where's intake?"

Ben frowned, looking from the uniform and then back to me. "I really, really think we should ask the receptionist—"

"Intake," I cut him off, waving a hand at him. "Don't play dumb—I know exactly who you are and who you work for. I'm an agent with the Sub Rosa Society, and you have five seconds to tell me where intake is before I signal my support team!"

I yelled this. I didn't mean to yell it, exactly, but as the words left my mouth, they climbed higher and higher until

I was shouting and shaking and angry. I didn't cut up a pair of pants and sneak a tray of cookies just to get stalled by two kids in an outdated training facility. My hands were clenched into fists, my eyebrows knitted together, and I glared at Beatrix, then Ben, then Beatrix again, until finally Ben spoke.

His voice was a little quieter now, more like his sister's. "I think you should lie down for a little bit."

"Show me where intake is!"

"Oh, we will!" Beatrix said earnestly. "In a second. Do you have blood-sugar problems? Lie down, and . . . Ben, how about you go get— Oh, good, he's already gone—" I turned to see the door of the gym swinging, marking Ben's exit.

This wasn't working. Even if these two weren't junior agents or agents in training, surely, whomever Ben went to get *was*—and I probably couldn't handle myself against a fully trained League operative. I shook my head, turned, and ran. I shoved through the gym doors and took a hard right, away from the way I came. The hall was echoey and bare, and I could hear Beatrix padding along behind me.

"Where are you going? Wait, come on—maybe we can talk about this!" she shouted. Her voice was getting farther away.

I looked over my shoulder—I was faster than she was.

This was crazy; I was *never* fastest.

But Beatrix was panting like she rarely ran, and her glasses kept slipping down her nose as she gasped behind me. I sped up, even though my overworked shins were cramping. There was a door ahead—unlabeled—but I didn't exactly have the time to worry. I smashed through it and into another hall similar to the one I just came through.

Beatrix was still behind me. I could feel the sweat slicking down my back. The stickers holding the sash together gave in. It fell to the floor.

Where are all the people? All the field agents? Their computer guys? Their analysts? A staircase ahead—I ran up it. When I looked back, Beatrix was still close behind, her hair fuzzy and cheeks blotchy red.

"Hey . . . look, he just went to get our uncle . . . You're not in trouble . . . How many stairs . . . Oh . . ." She was fading fast as we moved up the staircase.

In all honesty I was fading too, but I was fueled by the fear of failure—I had to find my parents today, because The League would inevitably be on even heavier lockdown after a breach. I flung open another door, spun, and pushed my back against it. I looked around; I was back on the main floor, by the offices I'd snuck through earlier. This was not good—even office people would notice if a Campfire Scout went tearing down their hallway.

I reached over and grabbed the red fire alarm, yanking it down.

A shrill blare ripped through the building.

No one moved. I heard a few people sigh and then

grumble about the alarm going off; one person rose and slammed her door.

Run, people! Why don't you run? I heard Beatrix's footsteps drawing closer and closer to the stairwell door.

I hadn't come this far to get caught. I looked for ideas. Above me was a copper sprinkler head. It had a little bit of red glass in the center—when broken, it would signal the water to start flowing. I knew this because of an unfortunate incident involving me, Walter, and our clever idea to build a full-size catapult in the SRS sparring ring.

I swung into the nearest office—where the guy was playing golf with a putter and a coffee cup. He stared at the fire alarm, frowning, like it was a radio turned up too loud. I shook my head at him, grabbed the putter from his hands, and ducked back out before he had a chance to react.

Beatrix pushed the stairwell door open just in time to see me swing the putter hard at the sprinkler head.

The sprinkler head cracked off the ceiling, breaking the red glass. Beatrix and I stared in unison for a brief second and then, just as the golf club owner whirled around his door, water began to gush down. The other sprinklers obediently kicked in.

Now, finally, there was action. Screaming, shouting, and squealing rang out. People dashed from their offices, papers or purses above their heads. From the end of the hall I could hear the receptionist shouting for people to "run for their lives!"

I questioned this receptionist's threat-response training.

I dropped the golf club and sprinted back toward the stairwell, brushing past Beatrix, who looked dumbfounded and maybe a little impressed. The door slammed behind me as I slogged upstairs, leaving a trail of puddle-footsteps. My street clothes were slowing me down; I shimmied out of them as I ran, darkly grateful for the waterproof SRS uniform underneath.

Now I needed a hiding spot—any hiding spot—where I could wait until I figured out where intake was. I reached the next floor and grabbed the door handle.

Locked.

I tried the next floor.

Also locked. Wheezing, I leaned back against the railing and looked straight up. The stairwell wound up and up and up above me so high, it made me dizzy.

The bottom door flung open and staring up at me were Ben, Beatrix, and two adults. One was tall and skinny and looked like a stretched-out version of Ben. The other was a tall blond woman wearing a pantsuit that was dripping water. She pointed to me.

"An SRS uniform, I see. Grab him, Clatterbuck," she said.

"Uh . . . okay," said the tall man—Clatterbuck, I guessed—sounding like he'd been woken from a nap and thought he might still be dreaming. He blinked back the water from his eyes and started toward me.

I swallowed. I couldn't even beat my own classmates in a fistfight. I didn't stand a chance against a real agent—much less a League agent. I tried not to look terrified as Clatterbuck approached. I had to say something, anything to stall them, to confuse them.

"Groundcover! I'm working on Project Groundcover!" I shouted, saying the first mission name that came to mind—the only mission name on my mind lately.

Behind Clatterbuck, the suit lady froze.

"What did you say?" she whispered. Clatterbuck stopped. He tried to look back at his boss without taking his eyes off me, which only caused his eyes to cross.

"Groundcover," I repeated, trying to puff my chest up. I deflated when the seams of my uniform sounded seconds from popping.

The suit lady smiled, the kind where it was all glossy lipstick lips and no teeth. She folded her hands at her waist.

"Relax, Clatterbuck," she said. Then to me: "Do you like pepperoni pizza?"

"I . . . what?"

"Pepperoni," the suit lady repeated. "We can order whatever you like. Just so long as you're telling us everything we want to know about Project Groundcover."

CHAPTER NINE

Clatterbuck was Beatrix and Ben's uncle. He didn't look impressive, but I opted to believe that he was—for all I knew, he was one of those assassin-type guys who could kill me with his pinkie or something. Those guys always looked weird. The suit lady didn't introduce herself, so it wasn't until they'd escorted me through the waterlogged hallway and back to her office that I read her name off the door: PAMELA OLEANDER: DIRECTOR OF OPERATIONS.

The League's director—its version of SRS's Dr. Fishburn. So, double terrifying.

Oleander sat behind her desk, where Clatterbuck had just set three boxes of pizza. Oleander opened up the nearest box, and steam rose from it. She lifted a slice and took a bite, dodging a few drops of grease just before they hit her pantsuit. Clatterbuck took the seat beside me and reached forward to steal a slice for himself. He mangled it into a lump of cheese and dough as he tried to open a can of soda without putting the pizza down.

Oleander chewed for a few moments before speaking. "Have a slice, Mr. . . ." She waited for me to fill in my name.

"Jordan. Hale Jordan," I said. The League *had* to know about my parents—I mean, everyone in the spy game had heard of Katie and Joseph Jordan. Maybe learning that *I* was a Jordan too would strike a little fear into their hearts.

Unfortunately, Oleander didn't react to the name. She just nodded and pushed the pizza box closer to me. I tensed the muscles in my stomach to keep it from growling. My vending machine breakfast had been ages ago, but no way was I taking any food The League offered me—it almost definitely had a sleeper drug in it.

Oleander shrugged when it became clear I wasn't taking a slice. "Mr. Jordan—let's be clear. I'm not offering you pizza after you flooded my building just to be nice. I'm doing it because I want your help."

I scoffed, but Oleander ignored it. She put her pizza down and leaned over the desk a little, keeping her eyes hard on mine. "I've heard of Project Groundcover. But I don't know what it entails. I want you to tell me."

I worked hard to look blank—I'd done well in Advanced Interrogation techniques and Body Language Analysis, so I knew Oleander was already making mental notes, working out what would make me crack. Best to give her as little information as possible. "You think I'll trade you information for some pizza? Not a chance. You have two of our agents," I said coolly. "Give them back, and we'll discuss Groundcover."

"I don't have them," Oleander said.

"I don't believe you," I answered.

Oleander sighed and put her piece of pizza down. "Mr. Jordan, even if I *wanted* to kidnap SRS agents, how would I go about it? Look around. Does this look like an elite spy agency to you? There's not a single field agent in this place, much less someone with the skill to take out two SRS agents. The government cut back our funding ages ago when we couldn't stop SRS."

I frowned. The League had government funding? That didn't make sense—SRS was the government organization. The League was the criminal agency. Why would criminals have government funding?

Oleander saw my hesitation and stopped on her way to grabbing another slice of pizza. She gave me a sort of pitying look. "Wait—that surprises you, doesn't it? I bet everything I'm saying surprises you. You've always been told that SRS are the good guys. That The League are the bad guys. Right? Of course you have."

I didn't answer.

"And you've probably been told we're huge and powerful and out to get you."

I still didn't answer, but I guess I didn't need to. Oleander rose. "Come with me," she said.

With Clatterbuck on my heels, Oleander walked me down the hall, past people mopping out their offices, and to the stairwell. She fumbled with a massive ring of keys that clinked together like an instrument as we walked up a flight of stairs to the very door I'd tried to open earlier. Oleander gave me a quick look and inserted a thick brass key into the lock, turning it.

The smell of age swept over me, old paper and blankets and stale bread. The floor was completely dark. Oleander stepped in first, the clack of her heels echoing across the room. She reached toward the wall and flicked the lights on. They protested, flickering and snapping as one by one they slowly lit.

"This was the tech floor, I think," Oleander said.

"No, this was the control deck," Clatterbuck said rather somberly, running a finger across a dust-caked desk.

"Sorry," Oleander answered. Then to me she said, "It was before my time. I didn't take over till after they'd pretty much shut everything down."

I barely heard this, too shocked by what I saw.

A control deck, similar to the one we had in SRS— dozens of desks, a gigantic screen, maps on the walls, speakers, a bridge lifted slightly above the rest of the room, like a stage, for the mission commander to pace on. Except everything in the room was wrong. It was old—the desks were empty, stripped of computers save a few yellow-gray monitors. The speakers on the walls were massive and square. Even the maps were wrong—countries and territories I'd memorized when I was nine were drawn in spots they no longer existed. It looked haunted, like a corpse of a room instead of a place where real people worked.

Don't fall for it. They made it look old. Nothing an effects team couldn't pull off while you were in Oleander's office.

"We're broken, Mr. Jordan. We're not powerful, we haven't kidnapped your agents, and moreover, we're not the bad guys. SRS is the place with high-end technology, with agents all over the world. I know they've convinced you that *they're* the secret government agency, but, well . . . it's not true. They lied."

"You're saying that SRS has managed to trick hundreds of agents, support staff, and their families into working for the wrong team? That's stupid," I snapped.

"That's genius," Oleander said steadily. "And furthermore, these agents who are missing? Look at The League. And then look at SRS. Which organization do you think has the resources to make two people vanish?"

"Are you saying SRS kidnapped their own agents?"

"I'm saying that's a lot more likely than us being behind it," Oleander said coolly. She retreated from the room, flicking the lights off as she went; one sparked as the fluorescent bulb blew. "We can continue the tour, if you want.

Seventy-nine floors total. I'll show you every one, if that'll make you believe me."

"It won't," I scoffed.

Oleander frowned at me; Clatterbuck looked back and forth between us like he was watching a tennis match. "Well then, Mr. Jordan," Oleander finally said. "Whatever will we do with you?"

I didn't realize it at the time, but Oleander was asking a real question—whatever would they do with me? Clatterbuck reported that the intake cells—they *did* have them, after all, which made me feel pretty smug—were full of storage boxes. Finally Oleander frowned and rapped a pen against her lips. "What's in your office, Clatterbuck?"

"Um . . . a chair, a desk, a bobblehead dog, a dead houseplant—"

"I mean, that he can steal or read or report back to SRS," Oleander said testily.

"Oh! Nothing. Everything on Creevy's been locked up," Clatterbuck answered. I didn't know who Creevy was, but I didn't want to let them in on that fact, so I stared at the wet floor like it was particularly interesting.

"All right." Oleander nodded. "We'll lock him in your office until he tells us about Groundcover."

"And if I never do?" I asked, folding my arms. I was trying to look menacing, but given the soaked SRS uniform, I suspected I looked more like a giant wet raisin.

Oleander gave me a pitying look. "You'll talk, eventually."

"Why would I do that?"

"Because," Oleander answered as she walked away, "you'll realize I'm telling the truth."

Truth.

She couldn't be—there was no way. And yet, that word shone like a beacon in my head, guiding me toward the last time I'd heard it. My parents, talking in the kitchen, my mom's voice on the edge of tears. *We pretend like we don't know the truth.*

Could this be the truth my parents were talking about?

Clatterbuck warily escorted me to his office, which was on the same floor as the gym and tucked away in a corner— as such it had been spared the sprinklers on the floor above. Being basement level, it didn't have a window, but he'd tacked a few dozen tropical calendar pictures to the back wall, which worked as a surprisingly decent substitute. Tropical pictures aside, the room looked like it belonged to a comic book illustrator, or maybe a zombie movie aficionado. There were vintage movie posters on the wall by the door and little figurines on every flat surface. Toy cars still in boxes and pictures of him with everyone from the Queen of England to that guy from the action movies. I couldn't help but think this office rivaled Kennedy's bedroom in terms of colors per square foot.

And it didn't look as evil as I'd expected for The League.

Clatterbuck gave me a sort of smile and turned to go, yanking a baseball player bobblehead off a shelf and tucking it safely into his pocket as he went. As soon as the door clicked, I sighed and collapsed into his desk chair, wiggling around as the edges of the duct tape covering the cushion poked me. My mind felt crowded, too many thoughts bumping into one another.

SRS agents were taught to trust our guts—it was the very first thing we learned when we started training at seven years old. Go with your first instinct and never look back. I'd always liked that—the idea that the right thing, the ground truth, was already deep inside us, and we just needed to listen to it. It was the lesson that convinced me not to give up when training got terrible, when Walter got muscles, when Kennedy became the best gymnast at SRS— because I always knew that deep down, the true thing in me was a spy, through and through, no matter how slowly I ran a mile.

But now, even while my head was shouting that Oleander must be lying, that The League was tricking me, the deep true thing was whispering, chanting over and over: *Truth. Truth. Truth.*

Find the truth.

CHAPTER TEN

I thought I was losing my mind—time seemed to be going in reverse. Then I realized time actually was going in reverse—that Clatterbuck had some sort of goofy backward clock. I shook my head at it, then continued to comb through his desk drawers. Most were full of Chinese menus and paper clips.

Someone rapped on the door. I eased the desk drawer shut and stood up gingerly.

"Hale?" a tiny female voice called out. "It's Beatrix. Beatrix Clatterbuck? From the gym?"

"I remember," I answered through the door.

"I brought you some pizza. My uncle said you didn't eat earlier."

"I don't want it," I answered, though again my stomach growled at that exact moment just to mock me.

"Okay," Beatrix said, sounding doubtful. "I didn't lick it. Seriously. Open the door."

"It's locked—"

"No, it isn't," Beatrix said. "I mean, it is, but it's locked from your side. They couldn't just lock you in forever; there's no bathroom."

She was right about there not being a bathroom, though it hadn't occurred to me till she'd said it. I strode to the door and pulled down on the handle; it clicked and the lock popped out obediently. I exhaled in disbelief—*they really had left me in an unlocked room?*—and pulled the door open. Beatrix grinned at me, and it was hard not to notice her overcrowded teeth. At SRS, she'd already be in braces. *Probably wearing contacts too*, I thought, looking at her pink-rimmed glasses. Agents couldn't risk losing their glasses in the middle of a mission.

A thin black net dropped from the ceiling over Beatrix's head.

Beatrix's eyes widened. She dropped the plate of pizza as the net whisked her off her feet. Limbs went everywhere as she was pulled up to the ceiling in a ball. The net's counterweight—another person—sank down, landing expertly in black SRS-issued boots.

With pink owl stickers on them.

"Kennedy?" I asked, wondering if perhaps I was hungrier than I'd thought. Was I hallucinating?

"Hale!" Kennedy squealed, bounding forward to give me

a hug, a flame of red hair bouncing around behind her. "I did it! The net trick! I wish I could tell Agent Hartman. She said I'd never get it before Darcy Bellows, but *look*!" My sister appeared to be either on the verge of tears or laughter, but it was impossible to tell which.

"Why am I in a net?" Beatrix asked from above. I looked up and saw that the net was slowly spinning side to side. Beatrix looked mildly inconvenienced, if anything. "That was the last of the pizza," she added, pointing to the plate that was now overturned on the floor.

"Are you all right?" Kennedy asked her, putting her hands on her hips. "It's my first net trap."

"I'm okay. Ben is going to be so mad I got caught in this instead of him—what sort of knot is at the top? I have to tell him. Did you use a pulley?" Beatrix asked.

"How did you get in here?" I asked.

"I shimmied through some windows downstairs. It was easier than I thought—apparently the building just flooded? Or caught fire? Everyone was too busy with that to notice me, I guess."

"Okay, okay, let's just get out of here," I said. I didn't want her to know, but I was pretty mad at her for following me— now I had to leave without answers about Mom and Dad, since there was no way I would let Kennedy stay here longer than necessary. "There are guards," I said swiftly as I stepped out into the hall beside her.

"League elites or just regular agents?" Kennedy asked.

"I . . . I don't think either," I said.

Kennedy didn't understand, but there was no time to explain. "You won't fit through the window I shimmied through to get in—"

"Emergency door," I interrupted. "First-level stairwell. I saw it earlier. It'll set off the fire alarm, but it's that or the front door. We'll have to run for it."

We froze in unison—footsteps, coming toward us from where the hall crossed up ahead, just in front of the 493 DAYS WITHOUT AN ACCIDENT! banner. Kennedy faltered. Sneaking into a building was one thing, but facing off with a League agent was another. She gave me a worried look—I had to move first. I was her big brother, after all. I rushed out into the hallway, shoes squealing on the floor. The footsteps belonged to three men who were running straight at us. I braced myself.

Kennedy leaped around me, flipped forward, and planted her foot squarely on the closest guy's chest. His eyes widened and he stumbled backward, but Kennedy didn't weigh enough to knock him down entirely. Kennedy whirled around to look at me smugly, nearly bonking herself in the face with her bright red ponytail. Two other guys started toward me. I jumped forward and grabbed the 493 DAYS WITHOUT AN ACCIDENT! banner. I yanked one end down, trailing the string that held it aloft behind me. I swallowed, then dived forward, sliding on the still-wet tiles toward Kennedy.

"The string!" I shouted, and she nodded. She wove it around the men's legs, then grabbed the bit of string that had held the banner up and wrapped it around the agents' feet as I heaved back to standing. The third guy, the one Kennedy had kicked, was watching everything, eyes wide, like he thought he might be hallucinating. Gritting my teeth, I ran straight for him, barreling into his chest. Kennedy didn't weigh enough to knock him over, but I certainly did—he stumbled backward and toward the other two, whose legs were now expertly laced together. I huffed another lap with the banner around the three until they were gathered together, wrapped up into the banner like a very odd bouquet. They shouted—at us, for backup, for whoever's-hand-is-on-my-butt-to-*move*-it.

Kennedy stepped back and grinned like she was admiring a glorious piece of art.

"Come on," I said, trying not to laugh—they did look pretty glorious, all things considered. Grabbing her hand, I pulled her toward the stairwell. I could hear more voices now. We burst into the stairwell, then through the emergency exit door.

The now-familiar fire alarm began to scream, but it didn't matter—we were out. We dodged through alleys and around buildings, pausing to take deep breaths. Most people didn't seem to notice us, but one kid stared at our uniforms, head cocked to the side, trying to work out what we were wearing.

"Scuba diving convention," I panted at him. We hurried off before he could remember we were nowhere near a body of water.

By the time we made it to the train, my legs felt like jelly. Kennedy, on the other hand, was bouncing, like she was drawing energy from the danger of it all.

"Did you see me, Hale? I totally got that guy!" Kennedy said, diving into the train seat.

I looked back the way we'd come, sure I was going to see a League agent running for us at any moment, but the city was normal. Busy, but normal. Still, I didn't take my eyes off the station platform until we'd rolled away and begun to pick up speed.

"Did you hear me, Hale?" Kennedy said, now whispering due to the full train, though it was the sort of whisper that might as well be a shout. "I bet if I keep doing the leg presses Agent Hartman's always moaning about, I'll be strong enough to knock him down next time!"

"Does anyone know you left?" I asked Kennedy.

She shrugged, tugging at the corner of her uniform. She'd managed to get a new one. "I don't think so."

"Does anyone know *I* left?"

"Just me. Because seriously, Hale, that was the worst fake-sick voice I've ever heard this morning. I knew you were up to something. So, did you find out anything? About where they're holding Mom and Dad? That's why you went, right?"

"That's why I went, but I couldn't find anything," I admitted, and I felt Kennedy tense with disappointment. I put an arm around her shoulders. "Don't worry, though. I'll figure something out."

It didn't take us long to walk back to the BR MBY COUNTY SUBSTITUTE MATHEMATICS TEACHER TRAINI G building. We pushed the door open together, then froze in the open frame.

A crowd was gathered at the receptionist's desk—Ms. Elma, Agent Otter, Dr. Fishburn, and a handful of agents—some of them my junior agent classmates. Otter, Green, and Kennedy's teacher, Agent Hartman, were all wearing SRS uniforms; Otter was stashing a switchblade in his pocket. My eyes widened. Seeing someone like Agent Otter preparing to go on an active mission was worrisome, because 1) it was a reminder my parents weren't available; 2) Agent Otter's uniform was three sizes too small, which was pretty horrifying; and 3) it meant Kennedy and I were in serious trouble, if they were sending senior agents after us.

"He's back?" one of the junior agents—it was Eleanor—whined. "Does this mean we don't get to go? Man . . ."

"Who cares?" Riley snorted. "I didn't want my first mission to be finding Fail Hale—"

Fishburn cleared his throat loudly, which shut the juniors up. He pointed at the elevator. Shooting me irritated glares, the juniors descended back into SRS.

Ms. Elma walked toward us in a slow, practiced way, like

a big cat. For a second I thought perhaps she planned on punching me—her scar seemed to be pulsing red, like some sort of anger beacon. The senior agents were behind her. Dr. Fishburn didn't get up; instead he leaned back in his chair and placed his fingertips together delicately.

The agents didn't seem to know exactly what to do when they reached us at the doors. We weren't family, so it's not like they could sweep us into relieved and happy hugs—and to be honest, the idea of Otter hugging me was sort of gross anyway. Kennedy, being much more precious than I was, got a brief and awkward side-squeeze from Agent Hartman.

"Where were you?" Agent Hartman asked. Her voice was rough but pretty. I always thought she looked like she should be playing acoustic guitar instead of spying.

"I wanted to go after Mom and Dad," I began, then paused. *Truth*.

"Jordan?" Otter asked, and I realized I'd been silent for too long.

"I wanted to go after Mom and Dad, but I got scared. I was hiding in the coffee shop." I tried to hold my eyes and lips still, since those are usually the things that gave liars away, while my stomach felt like it was boiling over into my lungs. We had an entire class on deception techniques, yet it hadn't prepared me for lying to the head of SRS.

"We checked the coffee shop," Fishburn said. He didn't sound mad. He didn't even sound doubtful. His voice was a straight line, no ups or downs.

"I was in the bathroom—"

"I checked the bathroom," Otter said, folding his arms.

"I was in the girls' bathroom," I said swiftly. The lie was getting easier as all the little untrue details fell into place in my head, like words in a book. "I got mixed up."

Otter frowned, turned to Kennedy. "Is that true?" he asked her.

Kennedy's face immediately broke into a wide grin. "Yep," she said smoothly. "I heard him crying through the door. It's the only reason *I* found him."

I tried not to glare at her addition to the lie. That said, her line about me crying did seem to convince the other two; Ms. Elma and Agent Hartman stepped back and turned toward Fishburn, who rose slowly. He didn't match the room; he was gray where it was brown, cool where it was warm. Fishburn sighed, walked over to me, and put a heavy hand on my shoulder.

"Hale," he said. "I know you're worried about your parents. We all are. But SRS has protocol in place for a reason. You can't just leave unsupervised. And you encouraged your sister to do it too! Lucky the downstairs receptionist saw her sneaking into the elevator, or we might have never known you two were gone."

I gave Kennedy a tense look. *Really, Kennedy? You went out the front door?* She chewed on her hair in response.

Fishburn shook his head, and then continued. "We did a full building lockdown for you two. But given that you're both under a lot of stress, and that no *real* harm was done, I'm going to let this breach slide. Kennedy, no gym privileges for a week . . . Hale . . ." I saw him debating what to do with me, since revoking my gym privileges was more of a gift than a punishment. He frowned. "Hale, janitorial duty for the week. And please, Hale, Kennedy—never again. Your parents being captured is a tragedy, not an excuse. Am I clear?"

"Yes, sir," Kennedy and I said in unison, Kennedy's lower lip trembling. I could count the number of times she'd been in trouble on . . . Well, actually, I couldn't count them. She'd never been in trouble.

"Ms. Elma, take them back home? And do keep a better watch on them this time," Fishburn said. Ms. Elma nodded curtly, and she put a hand around me. I think she was trying to be kind, but her nails dug into my arm as we got on the elevator and descended back into SRS headquarters.

"Here we go," Ms. Elma said as she unlocked the door to our apartment. "Back home, safe and sound."

I nodded and went to my bedroom. SRS was home, sure—it was where I'd grown up, after all. Apartment 300. Where my family lived, where I'd learned how to fake a Swedish accent and shot my first laser gun. It was where one day I'd (hopefully) become a field agent, where I'd eventually retire and maybe even teach the next generation of superspies.

SRS was home, but all I could think of right then was

what Mom and Dad said the morning they'd left—that heroes don't always look like heroes, and villains don't always look like villains.

I had to work out who was who. I had to work out the truth.

CHAPTER ELEVEN

The truth started with my parents. It was Oleander who gave me the idea, really—when she'd suggested that maybe SRS itself was behind my parents' disappearance. If that were true, there'd almost certainly be some sort of clue to it in Mom and Dad's personnel files. Everything got put in those, from if we'd had chicken pox to our favorite vegetables. Personnel files, of course, weren't available from any old SRS computer lab. If I had to guess, they were probably encrypted and accessible only by the computers on the control deck, which was always full of HITS guys. The HITS guys were relaxed, but they still wouldn't let me go poking around high-level encrypted files . . .

I needed help.

I was good at a lot of things. Russian, computer hacking, and putting on a disguise in under fifteen seconds, for example. I was not good at asking for help. There were a lot of reasons for this, but the main reason was: group projects.

Every so often Agent Otter would assign us fake missions we had to complete in groups of three or four—you know, stuff like "break open this door using four toothpicks" or "pretend I'm a League translator, and convince me you're my Bulgarian contact." No one wanted me on their team, so I usually got stuck with whoever was unlucky enough to have missed class the day everyone picked teams. Group projects at SRS were rarely about actually completing whatever the task was; they were about making the flashiest presentation. So while the other SRS kids in my group were figuring out ways to rappel into the classroom from the ceiling, I was actually opening the door or learning conversational Bulgarian. Mom always said I should talk to Otter about it; Dad said I should jam their rappelling equipment. I never did either—what was the point? I just wanted to get the dumb thing finished.

Anyhow, the point is, group projects didn't teach me how to work with a team. They taught me to trust no one.

But there *was* one person at SRS I could trust, and right now, I needed her. I kicked off my blankets and crept into the hallway. I poked my head into Kennedy's bedroom. The eyes of a dozen cheerleader animals stared at me, like they judged me for not wearing pink. I ignored them.

"Kennedy," I whispered.

"I'm getting up!" she shouted so loud that I dived for the bed and clamped a hand over her mouth. She jolted awake and almost screamed before realizing it was me. We both froze and stared at her bedroom door, cringing, waiting for Ms. Elma to barge in with her scar throbbing.

Nothing.

Slowly, I shut the door behind me. Kennedy's hair was tangled on top of her head, and her eyes were bleary and unfocused—I wasn't entirely sure she hadn't fallen back asleep.

"I need your help," I said quietly. "To figure out where Mom and Dad are." That was a partial lie, but it seemed safer this way.

"How?" she asked immediately.

"Are you really awake? You need to remember this."

"Yes!"

"What's seven times eight?"

"I don't know. I'm not good at math awake or asleep!" she answered, wrinkling her nose. "Seventy . . . fifty-six! It's fifty-six!"

"Right. Okay—I need the HITS guys out of the control deck tomorrow."

"When?"

"About two o'clock."

Kennedy looked at me solemnly for a few seconds, and then nodded. "Okay."

I knelt down by her bed and whispered quickly, explaining exactly what to do. She recited it all back to me four times before I nodded and stood.

"Are you sure you've got it?" I asked, warily. "We can go over it again."

She rolled her eyes and flopped back onto her blankets, curling them around her like a nest. "I've got it, Hale."

And then she was asleep again.

I wished it were that easy for me.

Truthfully, there were worse things than janitorial duty.

I mean, SRS didn't really get that *dirty*, since there wasn't much of an outdoor space. The janitors handed over a dustbin and broom and sent me off into the halls with instructions to come back once I'd swept all the way to the Disguise Department. Truthfully, they seemed pleased that I was in trouble—like they were proud of me for causing a little chaos.

"Except that lockdown," one of the janitors said in a thick Bosnian accent. "I was stuck off the cafeteria, by the garbage bins."

"*Žao mi je*," I said, which is "I'm sorry" in Bosnian. I didn't speak it as well as French and Russian, but I knew how to apologize and say, "I like your shirt"—which meant the janitors liked me way more than they liked any of my classmates. I wandered off, poking at the floor with the broom. The classrooms were on this hall; through a window I saw Walter doing pushups.

I wound through SRS, running the end of the broom along the baseboards until I finally arrived at the control deck. I glanced in, assessing.

Nine HITS guys, all with energy drinks or coffee cups on their desks. They were the only ones on deck when there wasn't a mission being run, and though I saw a few scrutinizing spreadsheets, most seemed to be playing video games. The gigantic screen in the front of the room blinked, updating the world map full of little light dots where active agents were. I wondered which—if any—were my parents.

Mission: Find out who's the hero
(and who's the villain)
Step 1: Get onto the control deck

"Hale!" one of the HITS called out. He waved to me, his fingers thick with dust from a tub of cheese puffs. "So, man. Yesterday."

"Yeah." I sighed, stepping into the doorway. "I dunno. It was just—"

Another HITS shook his head at me. "Hey, man, your parents are missing. It happens. They gave you janitorial duty?"

I smiled a little and nodded. I hated the fact that I didn't want to become a HITS guy—they were a thousand times nicer than Walter and four thousand times less sweaty.

"Want to take a break?" the first HITS guy said a little slyly. "Play a round of Starfighter?"

I grinned, then set my broom and dustbin by the door and walked over to one of the HITS guy's desks. He hurriedly closed a few windows on his screen, switched the settings over so I couldn't open any·files, and then offered me his chair.

"All right," one of them said, clicking something; suddenly the giant world map was replaced by the Starfighter opening sequence. I wasn't really good at the game, but they were, and I think they fully believed that one day I would give up and join them. And when that day came, I guess they wanted me to already be good at their favorite game.

"We got the expansion pack," one of the HITS guys explained.

"I thought you said it didn't come out for another few months?"

"It doesn't," he said with a wicked smile. "Come on, Hale. We're the tech guys at an elite spy organization, and you don't think we can break into Starfighter's servers?"

I laughed and forced myself to slouch and relax as we started up a game. I stole a glance at the clock every time we paused the game so they could take long swigs from their energy drinks/coffees. One fifty-three. *Come on, Kennedy.* I felt dumb worrying—this was the nine-year-old who broke into League headquarters. Surely she could handle sneaking out of class for *this*.

One fifty-seven. We started up another game and I began to lose faith—what if she'd been caught? She'd get punished again, and it would be my fault.

The intercom by the center computer beeped loudly, a light at the top flashing red. The HITS guys froze the game, the team leader cleared his throat, and the others sank down into their desks—throwing me out of my chair—like one big choreographed motion. They might be the HITS, but they were still trained by the SRS.

"HITS, how can we help?" the agent said quickly. The others were at their stations, poised and ready to act.

"Hi—can you guys come help me? I'm in the computer lab on level four and the whole thing is acting weird." My sister's voice was loud and so high-pitched, it made the speaker crackle.

Step 2: Create a diversion the HITS can't ignore

"Have you tried restarting?" the agent said as the others relaxed. They used the lull to ball up their empty chip bags and toss them toward the trash can. They all missed.

"Yeah, but it's just—okay, so I'm making a project on hypnosis for class with Agent Farley, and I wanted to make it pretty, so I downloaded all these free fonts off a website. And then this thing popped up that said I'd won a laptop, and I clicked it, and then—"

Again, like a dance number, the HITS jumped to their

feet. They sprinted for the door, their footsteps slapping down the hall so loudly, they sounded like a stampede. I heard them round the outside corner, shouting about virus protection and secure networks. It wouldn't take long before they sent someone back to watch the deck while the others performed software surgery on Kennedy's computer. I rushed across the eerily silent control deck and slid into the center computer desk—it was the one most likely to have full security clearance.

Step 3: Gather intel

First, Project Groundcover. It didn't take me long to figure out how to open case files—after all, I'd seen the HITS guys do it dozens of times.

Project Name: Groundcover
Status: Gold Level Classified

I groaned, louder than I'd intended—Gold Level meant only Dr. Fishburn could access it from his office computer. Still, I scrolled down. Most of the mission details were grayed out and unclickable. At the bottom, however, was a category that, while unclickable, still provided information that made me freeze for a dangerously long time.

Active Agents:
Katie Jordan (Role: RETINA SCAN REQUIRED TO ACCESS)
Joseph Jordan (Role: RETINA SCAN REQUIRED TO ACCESS)

There were other agents listed as well. A few were junior agents, but most were names I didn't recognize—I guessed they were probably from other SRS facilities. One was Alex Creevy, a name I vaguely remembered Clatterbuck mentioning back at The League—*Everything on Creevy was locked up ages ago*. I clicked on all the names uselessly, hoping to reveal more information, but finally the computer beeped angrily at me. If I kept this up, the entire thing might shut down—I had to keep moving. I closed the window, opened the index of SRS agents, and typed frantically.

Katie Jordan. Mom's file popped up, the borders of the window bright red to indicate the security clearance needed to access it. I heard something in the hall—maybe just the AC kicking on, maybe footsteps, but I didn't have time to pause and dwell on it. The computer slowed as the system struggled to pull up the hundreds of missions she'd participated in, Project Groundcover included. Meanwhile Dad's face appeared slightly smaller beneath hers, under the heading "Current Partner." Finally the computer caught up, and I scrolled down frantically. Status, status, I just needed to see her status. If SRS was telling the truth, she'd be listed as "missing in the field."

I froze, staring at the screen. Blinking, angry letters smashed through my eyes all the way to my brain, rummaged around, and tore up everything I thought was real.

Status: In the Weeds

Mom and Dad were marked to be eliminated on sight. By SRS.

CHAPTER TWELVE

You know that feeling when you're in the car, and you go over some little dip in the road, and your stomach goes up for just a second? At the moment you're a little scared because you feel all off balance, but once it's over, you realize it was pretty fun, and want to go over it again. But then the supervising agent driving you to the dentist is like, *No, we don't have time to go over bumps just for fun, Hale, now be quiet*?

Maybe that last part is just me.

But anyway, that feeling—like the world was dropping out from under you suddenly—that was what reading about my parents being In the Weeds felt like. The world fell away, and I kept waiting for that moment, the moment where someone revealed that this was all just a joke or a training mission or some sort of twisted test. I'd be embarrassed that I'd fallen for it, and my parents would come out and remind me that I should have kept my cool, and hug me, and then we'd go home and I'd complain about my uniform and we'd talk about blast-door-wiring schematics over dinner, like normal.

That didn't happen.

I printed the screen about my parents and kept the paper folded up in my pocket. Each time I took it out, I hoped it would read differently. Each time, I was more sure about what I had to do next: I had to *trust* The League. They'd told me the truth about my parents, so there was no reason to think they were lying about everything else. They were the heroes.

I had to go back. I had to become a hero too—for my parents' sakes.

For the next week I very, very carefully rebuilt my reputation—which is to say, I went back to being Fail Hale. There was too much attention on me, and I'd never be able to sneak away so long as that was the case. So, I went to class. I lost the race at the end. I avoided Walter and the Foreheads—who, given that I'd revealed their favorite kitchen escape route, were now especially Walter-y. I ignored Kennedy's concerned looks and Ms. Elma's attempts to convince us that she'd actually cooked dinner, even when we recognized the food from the cafeteria's lunch menu.

It paid off—the following Friday, Otter handed me his dry cleaning ticket and waved me off while Walter and the other junior agents headed to the firing range to practice defensive archery. I breezed past the receptionist, as per usual, but then instead of heading to the dry cleaner's, I boarded the first train to Fairview.

"Mr. Jordan! Dr. Oleander told me you might be back!" the guy at the reception desk said when I walked into League headquarters, and his voice was all flat—like he hadn't been *told*, but rather, *warned*. He kept an eye on me as he lifted his phone and pressed a few buttons, then spoke quickly into the receiver. A few moments later Oleander appeared at the end of the hallway, walking toward me quickly, pantsuit crisp and rustling.

"Mr. Jordan," Oleander said kindly, then held out a well-manicured hand. "I assume we have a lot to talk about."

I shook her hand, suddenly aware of how clammy my own was. "We do."

Oleander led me back to her office, where Clatterbuck joined us. I withdrew the printout on my parents and handed it to her.

"I broke into the control deck and saw that," I said quietly. "Katie Jordan and Joseph Jordan. Those are the two agents I thought The League kidnapped."

"*Jordan*—they're your parents, aren't they?" Oleander said, and I got the impression she wasn't entirely surprised.

I nodded. "I think they knew. About everything, I mean—I think that's why they were marked In the Weeds. They figured out that SRS were the bad guys."

Oleander exhaled. "Well, Hale, the news could be worse. They're In the Weeds, not Contained. That means they're on the run. SRS doesn't have them. And I'm guessing that also means that when you were here last time, you lied about being on a mission for Project Groundcover. You came on your own to rescue them, didn't you?"

I nodded again.

Oleander smiled a little. "That was very brave of you."

I didn't know how to answer, both because thanks seemed like a stupid thing to say, and because my chest felt like it was defrosting from how good it felt to hear someone say that. I waited a few moments before taking a breath and continuing. "I'm sorry I lied about Groundcover—but my parents really *were* working on that mission, whatever it is—that's what they were out on when they went missing. I'm sure if we can find them or make it safe for them to come to us, they'll tell you what they know. And in the meantime, I figure I can draw up blueprints of the SRS facility. I know you're low on people here, but I think with my blueprints, a fifteen-man team could get in there and cause enough damage to set them back. To really take them out, you'll need at least fifty people, and I don't . . . Well . . . I don't think we should hurt any of them. They're all probably just like me—they have no idea they're fighting for the bad guys. So we go back, get my sister, and then . . . I don't know, I guess we live here with you guys?"

"Mr. Jordan, that won't work," Oleander said delicately.

I stared. "Where are we going to live then?"

"Oh, no, I don't mean that—you're welcome to live in our dorms here, though everyone at The League actually lives off campus—Clatterbuck and the twins live in that beige apartment complex across the street? Never mind, that's not the point. What I meant was, we can't go into SRS at all. Not with fifty men, not with fifteen. Literally, we can't—we don't have the resources for a mission like that. We barely have the resources to keep the lights on. You're talking about putting our middle-age former field agents up against SRS's flawlessly trained army of . . . of . . ."

"Hard bodies," Clatterbuck offered, looking down at his belly mournfully.

Oleander looked annoyed, but she nodded. "Against SRS's very fit, very fast, very smart, very well-supplied agents. Hale, Groundcover is the pin in the middle of all this—I don't think it's just what your parents were working on when they went missing. I think Groundcover is *why* your parents went missing—or at the very least, it had to be what tipped them off about what sort of organization SRS really is. We have to know more."

I paused, trying not to be too bothered that there was someone else telling me to "think of the mission" instead of my parents. I guess directors of spy agencies are just mission-focused by nature. I said, "I don't know anything else. Groundcover is a highly classified mission. I can't access any information on it, and it doesn't sound like The League can either."

"But maybe together, we could," Oleander said.

"What do you mean?"

Oleander took a deep breath and glanced at Clatterbuck before responding. "We'd like you to go back to SRS. We'd like you to be a double agent. Keep working for SRS while really working for The League. If we figure out and stop Groundcover, not only have we kept SRS from becoming more powerful, but I think we're a lot closer to making it safe for your parents to come home."

Now it was my turn to take a deep breath. "Things don't work out well at SRS for double agents," I finally said grimly. I said agents, but I'd actually only ever heard of one double agent—it was supposed to be a secret, so naturally, everyone knew about it by the time we were seven. I'll spare you the finer points of what SRS did when they realized they had a traitor in-house. Let's just say that Kennedy swore she'd seen his ghost once.

"We know," Oleander said. "Don't think I'm oblivious as to what this would mean, Hale. But without an inside man, we're left exactly where we were before you broke in—"

"I didn't say I won't do it," I cut her off. "Just that things don't work out well for them. But yes—I'm in. I'll be a double agent."

Oleander looked pleased. She rapped her nails on the desk a bit and then spoke. "All right, Hale—what sort of missions are you on right now? What we need is to get you assigned to Project Groundcover, but we'll need to know—"

I lifted my eyebrows, halting her. "I don't go on missions."

"I'm sorry?"

"I don't go on missions," I repeated. "I can't pass the physical exam, so I'm not a junior agent."

Clatterbuck and Oleander gave each other wary looks. "Are you . . . close to passing it?" Clatterbuck asked hesitantly.

"No," I answered. "Look, I'll do what you want—but there's no way they're going to start sending me on missions."

Oleander frowned. "Well. Huh. Clatterbuck? Any ideas? What would you have done back in your mission days?"

"We would've sent in a different agent," Clatterbuck said uselessly. "How is a kid able to break into *and* out of League headquarters not a junior agent?"

"Your security isn't very good," I muttered. Clatterbuck looked offended, but Oleander sort of nodded in agreement and then sighed.

"Hale, why don't you head to the cafeteria and grab some dinner while we sort this out?"

"All right," I said. "But I've got to be back at SRS before lockdown at seven, or they'll miss me." I trudged down to the cafeteria, hands slung in my pockets.

I wasn't quite sure why The League called this a

cafeteria—it was really a wall of vending machines and a basket of sandwiches made from questionable-looking cheeses. There wasn't an attendant, but there was a jarful of coins and a sign that said HONOR SYSTEM. I didn't have any money, and I didn't think it'd bode well for me to take one without paying—after all, that would mean my first act at The League was to flood the place, and my second was to steal. There was a little bowl of candy on one of the chipped-up tables, though, so I slumped down into one of the closest chairs and ate one.

"Hale!" someone said cheerily. I looked up to see Ben walking into the room, followed by Beatrix. "You came back!"

"I did," I answered.

"Did you sneak in? Did you use another disguise?" Beatrix asked excitedly. "Ben and I were talking about that Campfire Scout uniform—well, actually, everyone was talking about it. That was genius. *Genius.*"

"It was just some cut-up pants," I said, though I did feel myself swell a little. That outfit was pretty clever, and I knew it. "But no, I didn't sneak in. I came to talk to Oleander. She was right. SRS has my parents marked In the Weeds. I snuck into the HITS room and looked up their files. But now they want me to go rogue and be a double agent—" I stopped, because I realized Ben and Beatrix were staring at me, wide-eyed.

I really had no idea how to talk to kids who weren't spies.

Ben sat down on the tabletop, swinging his legs off the edge. Beatrix took the spot across from me.

"So, is it like in the movies? Do you know karate? I took karate once, but I wasn't very good," Ben said. I opened my mouth to answer, but he kept on going. "I bet it's *just* like the movies. Do you walk away from a lot of explosions?"

"What?" I asked.

"You know. Something explodes and you just walk away. Because you don't even care. You're that cool. *Walk away.*"

"Uh, no. I don't think I've ever walked away from an explosion," I said.

"Have you ever killed anyone?" Beatrix asked hesitantly.

"What? No. We're spies, not assassins!" I answered.

Ben changed the subject, sort of, which I appreciated. "So you're going to be a double agent? You're going to spy on SRS?"

"I *was* going to. But Clatterbuck and Oleander's plans all revolve around me getting sent on missions, and I'm not a junior agent."

I reached forward to take another candy out of the bowl. They were purple, so I imagined they were supposed to be grape, but they tasted a little strange. Beatrix made a yelping noise and dived for my hand.

"Have you been eating those?" Ben said, and his tone was urgent. Urgent enough that I realized we were talking about something more serious than a broken honor system.

"Yes—well, I ate one," I said, lifting my eyes. Beatrix,

who was clutching my forearm halfway to the candy dish, made a whistling sound through her teeth.

"That's not good," Ben said.

"What? Wait, is it poison? *Why is it out in the open?* No, never mind that—*antidote*. Get me the antidote, and hurry," I said through pursed lips. I wanted to shout that, of course, but I knew from Intro to Chemical Compounds that panicking would make my heart race, which would just get the poison into my system even faster. I took a deep breath.

"It's not poison," Ben said. "Don't worry. It's one of my inventions."

I let the breath out. "You invented hard candies?"

"Not *all* the hard candies. Just these specifically. They're called JellyBENs."

"JellyBENs?"

"I put my name in everything I invent. That way no one can rip me off. Ever heard of Nikola Tesla?"

"I think so . . . ," I said.

"Well, he invented the radio, but who got credit for it? Marconi. All he did was steal the idea, and suddenly, oh, thanks, Marconi, your invention is totally revolutionizing communication! Tesla should've gotten that award. And don't even get me started on Niagara Falls—did you know that Edison totally ripped Tesla off? He promised to pay him . . ." Ben ranted, throwing his hands around.

Beatrix gave me a sympathetic look. "Ben gets very upset about Tesla."

"Clearly," I said. "So what do JellyBENs do, exactly?"

"Well," Ben said, frowning. "They're *supposed* to have a side effect. But . . . Beatrix, shouldn't it have happened by now?"

"That's what my notes say," Beatrix answered, looking down at her Right Hand. "Hang on—no! We have to account for his height and weight—"

"There!" Ben said, pointing enthusiastically at me.

I frowned and looked at my hands. Nothing was happening. Beatrix finally pressed a few buttons on her Right Hand and held the screen up to me. She'd flipped the camera so I could see myself on the screen—my entire face was purple.

Not like, oh-is-he-choking? purple. Really, really purple—the sort of color you'd expect to see on rare Amazonian frogs. The color of the kittens on the walls in Kennedy's bedroom. Bright, obnoxious purple.

"Ben, Beatrix," I said calmly. "Why is my head purple?"

"Oh, it's not just your head," Ben said. "It'll spread to your chest— Oh, I think it already has! Wait, is your butt purple yet?"

"I haven't checked," I said. "How long will this last? Because I have to go back to SRS tonight."

Beatrix shrugged. "Since you only ate one, the color should fade in an hour or so. Now, if you'd eaten *all* of them, you'd be purple till . . . I'd say next Thursday?"

"At least," Ben agreed. "Beatrix was purple for almost

three days, but you weigh more than she does, so you'll burn the chemicals off faster."

I exhaled. Somehow the inside of my mouth tasted purple. "All right, all right. How'd you learn to do this, anyway? Does The League teach classes like SRS does?"

"Classes? No—Beatrix and I are homeschooled through the Internet. But I didn't exactly *learn* how to do this—I found some leftover chemicals in dry storage and started inventing things."

"So . . . that's what you do all day? You mix chemicals?"

"No! Of course not. Some days we just rewire things," Beatrix said, looking offended. "Sometimes it's just for fun, but the JellyBENs . . . We thought maybe someone would like them for April Fools'. You know, 'Turn all your friends purple!' and—"

"That's it!" I cut her off. I looked at the bowl of JellyBENs, then back up at them. I grinned.

"Oh, his teeth are purple too!" Beatrix exclaimed, and typed this into her Right Hand.

"Guys," I said, "I've got an idea for these, and it has nothing to do with April Fools'."

CHAPTER THIRTEEN

I un-purpled a little bit later and left The League with my pockets jammed full of JellyBENs. I thought about explaining the plan to Clatterbuck and Oleander, but I ended up keeping my mouth shut since, for one, I figured Ben probably wasn't supposed to be playing around with expired chemicals and second, if the whole plan failed miserably, I didn't want them losing even more hope in my double-agent abilities.

"Don't worry, Hale," Clatterbuck told me as we drove back toward SRS. I was in the backseat of a beat-up Chevy, hunched down under a blanket just in case someone from SRS happened to glance into the car. "Oleander and I will figure something out. I've just got to get back into the agent mindset, you know? Make my mind all steely again." He thumped his temple as he said that. "I tell you, Hale, I was one of the elite back in the day. Where should I drop you?"

"The dry cleaning place, if you don't mind—have to get Agent Otter's jackets. Do you have five dollars? I spent the money they gave me for dry cleaning on train fare."

"I'm sure I've got something. The train isn't going to work forever though—what if you need to come to see us and there's not a train leaving anytime soon?"

"True," I said. "Plus, that sort of regularity is risky. We need to mix it up. Maybe you could drive a different car and come get me, next time?"

Clatterbuck's face lit up, and I couldn't exactly figure out why. "Yes! Yes, I can do that. You know, I was just about to start doing international field work, but then, well . . . then I sorta had to take in Beatrix and Ben, which meant retiring . . ."

I frowned. "Why'd you take them in? Where are their parents?"

Clatterbuck sort of shifted in his seat. "They were field agents too. Beatrix and Ben were only three. They don't remember much, fortunately."

I lay very still, though my stomach was flipping over and over in my gut. I wanted to know how, when, *why*, but all the questions in my head sounded prying. I was grateful when Clatterbuck finally eased the car to a stop and turned around to face me. I pulled the blanket off my head but stayed down low.

Clatterbuck smiled, shaking off at least the most obvious bits of sadness over Ben and Beatrix's parents. "Right, here you go—four dollars and sixty-seven cents is all the cash I have on me. But I do have *this* for you," he said, and extended his closed fist with a grin. He stuck his hand right under my nose and then opened his palm dramatically, revealing a thick gold bangle with a large ruby in the center.

"You got me a pretty bracelet?"

"It's a communication unit!" Clatterbuck said brightly.

"Is it?" I didn't mean to sound doubtful. It was just that the thing was massive compared to the coms we used at SRS. Plus? It was all . . . sparkly.

"Oh, come on, just hide it under your sleeve," Clatterbuck said, reaching forward and slipping the bracelet—I meant, com unit—over my wrist. I sighed. At least if Walter and his friends saw it, they'd be too busy laughing to realize I was double-crossing SRS. Clatterbuck continued, "That's just the microphone—it doesn't have great range, but we can pick up conversations within a few feet. The earpiece . . . Well . . . you don't have to *wear* it all the time. Just put it on when you want to talk with us." He reached into his vest pocket and removed a heavy-looking ruby earring. The clip-on kind, the sort that was too fancy and overdone to possibly be a real jewel.

"You have got to be kidding me."

"Now, come on, Hale. This is the only com unit we have that'll work from underground. Actually, it's the only one we have that still works, period. All the others had dead batteries and I couldn't figure out how to change them out. Only one earring is an earpiece, but there's a second—hang on, it's down deep in my pocket . . . Oh, there it is. Anyway, there's a second so they look like a set of earrings. You'd look stupid just wearing one earring, after all."

"And I definitely wouldn't want to look stupid," I muttered, plucking the earrings from his fingers.

"I've got a set too, only mine are emeralds. I promise you, Hale, I'll be wearing them all the time just in case you need us. All the time."

"Even in the shower?" I said, grimacing. I didn't like to think of talking to Clatterbuck in the shower. I liked the idea much less when I realized he'd not only be in the shower, but wearing ladies' jewelry.

"Well, no. They aren't waterproof. I know! I won't shower until I hear from you!" He nodded at me sincerely.

"Thanks," I said, and weirdly enough, I was grateful. It wasn't every day I saw someone so dedicated to talking with me. I jumped out of the car and cut around the back of the building. It took only a few moments to grab Otter's dry cleaning and slide back into SRS headquarters.

"You missed it!" Kennedy said when I walked into our apartment. Her volume told me that Ms. Elma wasn't around, which was a relief. She was still pretty mad at me over the lack of Present-Palooza a few weeks back.

"Missed what?" I asked.

"We did a field exam today," Kennedy said, hopping from one foot to the other. "And my teacher says I can maybe test for junior agent later this month!"

My mouth dropped. All I could see were our parents' names beside the status "In the Weeds." How could Kennedy still be excited about being an agent for SRS?

Because she didn't know.

I didn't feel good about it, but I lied to Kennedy. After I got back from the HITS lab, I told her I couldn't find anything. I told myself this was because I was worried she couldn't keep it a secret, but really, it was because I just couldn't handle telling my sister that our home, our school, our *world* wanted our parents killed. It was just too much. She was only nine, after all.

"Congratulations," I said. I walked to the couch and flopped down next to her. "I'm sure you'll pass. You'll be a great junior agent."

This was true—I was sure she would pass. And I was sure she would be a great junior agent.

Which terrified me.

Timing is everything to a spy.

One second too early, you get spotted. One second too late, you miss a brush pass. I didn't just need the right second, though—I needed the right *day*.

The trouble was, agents—especially junior agents—didn't typically get a lot of lead time on missions. My parents were usually notified the day of for a domestic mission; for an international mission, if they were lucky, they might get twenty-four-hours' notice. It made sense for Fishburn to keep information close—he often said, "The more moving parts, the more things there are to break." Too many people involved with mission details, and there was too big a chance of something accidentally getting leaked or discovered or hacked and wrecking the entire thing.

So, I had to wait.

"No double cuts, and if it blows, you start over," Otter barked at us on Friday, like we'd offended him just by showing up for class. We were diffusing mock bombs, and I was pleased to see Walter was failing miserably. His bomb blew up three times before I'd even begun, largely because he wasn't taking the time to work out how it was wired—he was just hacking and hoping for the best. Luckily for him, these weren't actual explosives—they were just computer programs that flashed the word "boom" at you and played a cheesy exploding sound if you messed up.

The fake bomb in front of me had a half dozen wires strung between the cylinders of metal. The wires were a mess—tangled and knotted together, and the ends were stripped of their colors so that you couldn't always tell which color wire really was connected to what. A timer had been fixed to it, which was new to us, and it made the whole diffusing thing a whole lot harder.

Walter blew up again.

I inched my fingers into the bomb, reaching for the pink wire that was lodged down by the bottom. That controlled the bulk of the device, so surely it was a good place to start. I reached in and clipped it. Nothing happened. I grinned and turned to look at the timer . . .

I blew up.

"Oops," said Michael—one of the Foreheads. "Butterfingers, Hale?" Walter snorted in response and the two of them did some sort of handshake that involved both chest- and fist-bumping.

"Butterfingers? Nope," I muttered, clipping a different wire. I paused.

It didn't blow.

My computer screen turned bright green. I pushed my chair back and folded my arms.

"Don't look so happy with yourself," Walter told me. "Come next Friday, you'll still be here, making latte runs while I'm in the field on an actual *mission*."

"What, like interviewing kids at a chess championship?" I muttered under my breath. Walter's first junior agent mission had been a few months back, and it hadn't exactly been a riveting page-turner.

Walter glowered but didn't say anything else. Instead he cut another wire and his screen turned green. It was only a moment later that most of the class's screens did. Cameron, the other Forehead, was last. I thought it was pretty ridiculous that no one got mocked for coming in last place *here*. Otter walked to the main computer and typed in a few things; our bombs reset, with different parameters this time, and we began again.

I beat my classmates every time, but I hardly noticed. My mind was on the mission—my mission for The League. But moreover, whatever mission Walter planned on going on next Friday.

Walter wouldn't be going. But if everything went perfectly, *I* would be.

CHAPTER FOURTEEN

While most everyone at SRS ate dinner in their apartments, lunch was pretty much always eaten in the cafeteria. No one wanted to run back to their apartments, eat, and then rush back to class or work or Central Asia, so everyone was willing to muddle through whatever super-healthy and super-tasteless combination of foods the nutritionists had drummed up. After Thursday's morning classes—during which Walter managed to take his shirt off not once, but twice—we all walked to the lunchroom in a pack, Otter trailing along behind us. I kept pace with the others. Then, when we cleared the cafeteria doors, I hurried ahead in the line.

Mission: Get sent on Friday's mission
Step 1: Wait for chili day

Four-bean chili was famous at SRS, because it was the closest thing the nutritionist would make to junk food. Sure, it was meatless and cheeseless, and the nutritionist was always trying to convince you that soft tofu was a perfect topping, but *still*. In a sea of salads and fish cakes, chili was precious. No one missed getting at least one bowlful.

Today was chili day.

A few ladies from Enemy Surveillance were already eating but rose when we jostled our way toward the soup station. They looked annoyed that a bunch of kids were interrupting their lunch break. I got to the serving counter first, grabbed a bowl, and reached for the ladle. Cameron pressed in close behind me, like if he didn't practically stand on my shoulder bones, he might miss out.

Step 2: Force proximity

Proximity was key for this sort of trick. The closer you were to someone, the less they could see. Everyone knew that—in fact, everyone at SRS knew this *entire* trick, since we learned it in year three. But since it didn't involve explosions, daring escapes, or fancy codes, I suspected my classmates wouldn't even realize I was pulling one over on them.

"Back off," I huffed at him, taking my time lifting the lid from the pot of chili.

"Come on, Hale," Cameron said, rolling his eyes at me. "You're holding everyone up."

Step 3: Create a diversion

I lowered the ladle into the chili, scooped up a serving, and brought it toward my bowl. I let the ladle strike the side of the pot, spilling about half of its contents over the edge and onto the floor. Cameron behind me jerked backward so the splatter didn't get him, forcing those behind him to do the same.

"Careful, man!" he shouted, and a few of the people in the back of the line craned their necks to see what the holdup was all about.

"It's your fault! You're right on top of me. What's your problem?" I said, trying to puff myself up the way Otter did when he was angry (take a moment to be as freaked out as I was to be acting like Otter *on purpose*). Cameron's eyes jolted from the ground to mine, challenging me. Which meant I had the last thing I needed to pull this off.

Step 4: Get their attention

You couldn't keep your eyes on someone *and* on the giant vat of chili.

"That was rude. You should apologize," Cameron said

threateningly. At this, the line behind him went silent. I hesitated.

"Whatever. Fine. I'm sorry," I said swiftly. Then I broke our eye contact and returned the ladle to the chili, scooping up a small bowlful. I hurried to grab a seat while the rest of the class filed through the line. Otter finished flirting with the nutritionist and followed behind them. Soon the other classes started filing in—the eleven-year-olds, then the ten-years-olds, and then Kennedy's class of nine-year-olds. They all took big bowlfuls of chili.

Step 5: Everyone enjoys four-bean chili

Well, technically, it was now *five*-bean chili, since I'd managed to dump nearly the entire bag of JellyBENs into the vat during the diversion. They sank down into the chili while I held eye contact with Cameron. And now they were being eaten by every single person at SRS. Including me.

I dug my spoon in and took a few bites. I could taste the bright flavor of the JellyBENs, but only because I was looking for it. I lifted my eyes to make sure the rest of my classmates were eating as enthusiastically as expected on chili day. They were; in fact, some were nearly finished with their first serving. So far, this was going perfectly. I just hoped there were enough that everyone got at least one.

Someone screamed.

It was a junior agent, a girl from my class with pretty

hair. Personally, I thought her hair looked even prettier complimented by the lavender shade her skin was turning, but based on the horrified looks she was giving her ever-purpling palms, she disagreed.

"Is she choking?" someone shouted.

"Does she need mouth-to-mouth?" Michael shouted louder.

"Don't you dare!" the girl shrieked back. "What's happening? What—"

Another shriek. This time from a boy a year younger than I was, who was now the sort of flat color of squashed plums. Then Michael himself turned, then Otter, then . . .

I looked down and suppressed a grin. My hands were turning a now-familiar shade of violet.

Step 6: Everyone turns purple

Someone went running to get the on-call nurses, who then ran in with bags full of shots and wraps and pills, none of which were especially useful against a plague of purple. They sealed off the doors, just in case whatever we had was contagious, but it didn't take long for everyone to figure out that whatever it was, it had to do with the food. The nurses picked through the remains of the chili vat, but it was mostly empty. When they looked at the pot the nutritionist had been moments from bringing out, they found nothing but four kinds of regular old beans swimming in a thick broth. Still, they took samples, which they passed off to a few agents from chem lab for testing.

"I told Dr. Fishburn! I told him to stop getting chemical shipments through the kitchen doors! This was bound to happen! *Bound to happen!*" the nutritionist cried as she flipped through her recipe book frantically, like she'd somehow missed a note that warned "may cause purple." I felt a little bad about how upset she was, but given how often she tried to pass off cucumbers as a dessert item, my guilt didn't last long. I sat back. A few people had apparently missed out on getting a JellyBEN in their chili—but luckily for me, they were mostly the nine-year-olds. Otter was a particularly rotten-looking color, but oddly, it suited him, though he looked a little bit like a walking tomato as he frantically talked to Fishburn over a com unit.

"Hale!" someone shouted beside me. I spun around—it was Kennedy, who was almost neon purple. Added to her bright red hair, she looked like some kind of exotic flower.

"Don't worry, Kennedy—" I began, but Kennedy cut me off with a big grin.

"I'm not worried! This is awesome! Hey—wait. Yours is fading!"

"Huh?"

Kennedy motioned at me, and I looked down. Sure enough, the purple was fading slowly, just like it had back at The League. First my nose, then my cheeks and ears. It was another two hours before the color was gone entirely, but by the time they let us out of the cafeteria, I was completely normal-colored. The nurses swarmed me.

"Huh," said the oldest nurse, a woman with wispy gray hair and big glasses. "I guess he metabolized it quicker. Makes sense—he's a bigger guy than the rest of them."

"You're saying Hale isn't purple anymore because he's Hale the Whale?" Walter asked, laughing.

I lifted an eyebrow at him. "You look like an Easter egg, and you're making fun of *me*?"

Walter sniggled to a stop and rolled his eyes, but I saw his ego deflate a little. It was very satisfying.

Walter and the other purple people walked out of the cafeteria.

Otter stepped though the crowd. I hadn't even realized he was still here. "Hale! Dr. Fishburn and I will need to talk with you. His office, thirty minutes."

"Yes, sir," I said, nodding. It was hard not to grin—my plan was working.

I walked Kennedy back to our apartment, where Ms. Elma was waiting for us. She didn't believe in taking lunch breaks, so she'd been spared the whole incident. She acted like Kennedy hadn't tried hard enough *not* to turn purple. I made it back to Fishburn's office just a few moments early and sat down by the door, leaning my back against the sleek frosted glass that made up the administrative sector. I could hear Fishburn talking with someone—I think the nutritionist?—on the other side.

Down the hall, another door opened. I leaned forward to see who it was, then tightened my chest to hold in a groan. Mrs. Quaddlebaum, wearing a suit so stiff that it looked a little like a beetle's shell. She gave me a firm stare as she passed, clutching several folders to her chest. She was the assistant director—did she know about my parents being In the Weeds? Did she know that SRS was really the criminal organization? It was impossible to tell.

Walter was just behind his mom. His skin was a particularly feminine shade of purple, like the color of fancy eye makeup or expensive flowers. Walter scowled at me and continued on after his mother; just as he reached the door that led out of the administrative sector, he stopped. I saw him argue with himself for a moment, looking at the ceiling and tapping his toes. Eventually, he glanced over his shoulder at me.

"Uh, I'm . . . I'm real sorry to hear about your parents, Hale," he said swiftly.

"Thanks." It wasn't until the word left my mouth that I realized I was saying it, and it hung in the air between us, inflated by ten years of being friends and one of being mortal enemies. It felt like one of us should say something else, but what? We'd already fought about Walter ditching me. We'd had shouting match after shouting match about how "people change" and "it's not like we *wanted* to be best friends, we just ended up that way."

So there was nothing left, really. Walter pulled open the door and shut it behind him.

I puzzled in the quiet for a second, but then the door to Fishburn's office swung open. The nutritionist stepped out cradling her cookbooks and sniffling to herself. I rose and walked in; Otter was sitting in a chair by Fishburn's desk.

"Sit down," Otter said, rubbing his temples like he couldn't bear to look at me.

I lowered myself into one of the metal chairs across from Fishburn's desk. It wasn't until I was sitting down that I felt my stomach drop a little. They weren't just Otter and Fishburn, my teacher and director, anymore. Now they were Otter and Fishburn, my . . . enemies? That word seemed too strong, but it was true. Otter might've been too low-ranking to know my parents were In the Weeds, but Fishburn definitely knew. Fishburn was the one who'd called for it, in fact—he was the director, after all. How could he? This was his fault, everything was his fault . . .

I took a sharp breath and forced my thoughts to a halt. If I let my emotions get the best of me, Otter and Fishburn would see it on my face, and my whole plan would be ruined.

"Hale," Fishburn said carefully as he rolled his fingers across a pencil. "As you know, today we had a little bit of . . . what would you call it, Agent Otter?"

"Pandemonium? A total breakdown of a basic ordering-and-delivery system? A potential poisoning—"

135

"Drama," Fishburn said tartly. "Let's say we had a bit of drama today in the cafeteria." Fishburn paused to double-check that the pencils on his desk were all lined up correctly. "We had a mission scheduled for tomorrow morning—an important one, one that only a junior agent can help with. But from the looks of things, whatever *drama* happened in the cafeteria today has turned all our junior agents purple. We can't exactly send purple people on a mission. They'd attract all sorts of attention."

"Right."

"So, we've changed a few of the parameters and stream-lined things. And we would like you to go instead."

Step 7: Become the last resort

I blinked. I mean, this was what I'd wanted. This was what I'd planned for. Yet actually hearing Fishburn *say* it? My mind felt all blank and soggy. I stared. I knew my mouth was hanging open, but I couldn't remember how to shut it.

"To be clear, you're not a junior agent. We just don't want to scrap the mission—it's really very simple, anyway. Planting a small bit of software onto the computers at a children's hospital. We've got a folder for you here." He paused to lift a blue folder from his desk and hand it to me. "Tomorrow, zero eight hundred, you'll meet Agent Otter by the eleva-tors. Okay?"

"Got it," I said.

Fishburn gave me a kind smile, but it was a little forced. Otter didn't bother trying; instead he sucked at his teeth and shook his head. I thanked them both a few times, then left. Once I was alone in the hallway, I took a big breath and closed my eyes. A balloon had been inflating in my stomach, and now it felt like it was going to burst out of my chest.

Finally I was being sent on a mission. A real mission, not some stupid errand. I was being trusted, I was a spy, a real spy, and now everyone would know it. I thought about how Kennedy would react, how Mom and Dad would react . . .

The balloon in my stomach deflated. I'd imagined this day hundreds and hundreds of times before—literally dreamed about it, even. And in every single version, I ran home to tell my parents. They celebrated and cheered and beamed like the sun and brought out ice cream and told me, *We always knew you could do it, Hale!* In every single version, I was working for the good guys, not the criminals.

This wasn't the way I'd planned on it happening.

But real spies can deal with a change of plans.

As expected, Kennedy lost her mind when she heard the news of the mission. She bounded and rebounded off all the furniture, talking quickly about how excited she was, how excited I should be, had I thought about what form of martial arts I would use? Had SRS provided me with a cover character? Because if not, she could help me think of one. Ms. Elma regarded Kennedy's enthusiasm with a horrified look, like my sister was some sort of lab experiment gone wrong—though that might have just been because she was still a little lavender around the ears.

Eventually Kennedy's boiling glee reduced to a simmer. I said I was going to study the folder of mission details, then go to sleep early—I had to be up at zero eight hundred, after all. That was partially true—I *did* study the mission details, going over them again and again. I didn't, however, go to sleep early. I listened to Kennedy go to bed, then Ms. Elma creak down the hall to my parents' bedroom, where I didn't like to think about her sleeping. It was only then that I opened my bedroom door to retrieve the League com unit.

It's hard to hide things in a building full of spies, especially when one such spy is your kid sister who isn't afraid to mess with your stuff. Plus, I didn't trust Ms. Elma not to snoop around in my room while I was away in class. *But* . . . there was a linen closet directly opposite my bedroom, full of towels and sheets but also full of fat winter blankets that we wouldn't need anytime soon. I'd carefully tucked the jewelry away in the folds of the largest one; I darted my hand between the folds, retrieved the com, and—feeling somewhat smug about my hiding spot—went back to my bedroom. I holed myself up in my closet with the com and the mission folder Fishburn had given me, then lifted the earring to my ear. I could hear faint static through it.

"Clatterbuck," I whispered into the bracelet's enormous ruby centerpiece. "It's me." I began to wish we'd come up with call names on the odd chance someone at SRS was hacking into the com.

"Hale? Hale?" Clatterbuck said on the other end almost immediately. "Hold on, my earring isn't on right."

There was a rustling sound. When it stopped, I continued. "I'm going on a mission tomorrow," I said.

Clatterbuck's voice was loud now, so loud that I worried this ancient com unit had some sort of speakerphone setting. "Really? What kind of mission?"

"It's not for Groundcover," I said with a sigh—that'd been the first thing I'd checked for in the folder. "It's part of something called Operation Evergreen. Another agent and I are going to a children's hospital in Fairview—I'll be undercover as a sick kid named Clifton Harris, and another agent will be playing my father. The objective is for us to install a program on the hospital's servers."

"Like a . . . like a computer program?" Clatterbuck said. He sounded like he was trying to speak a foreign language.

"Yes! Of course. I don't know what it does, though. I mean, I can't see them intentionally crashing the servers in a children's hospital, but—"

"Hale?" a new voice said. I frowned, confused for a moment.

"Beatrix?" I asked.

"Hey. My uncle isn't really a computer person—he was

an agent back when computers were the size of a suitcase, you know? But I can help you."

"How?"

"I can write a program to go on top of whatever they've created. I'm guessing they'll have it on a flash drive, right?" Beatrix's voice was bright and cheery, like we were talking about sharing a photo collection.

"I'm leaving at zero eight hundred. There's no time to write a program."

Beatrix made a little noise of indignation, and I heard her lean away from the receiver—from the bracelet, I guess. "He thinks I can't write one before eight in the morning! I *know!*" She was back and loud in my ear. "I can write the program; I just need to figure out how the children's hospital wrote *their* program, and then figure out what the most obvious way would be for SRS to write *their* program, and then reverse. You know what? Just . . . I can do it. It'll be ready by eight."

I wasn't totally convinced, but seeing as how her brother had already proven himself a pretty excellent inventor, I had no reason to think Beatrix wasn't equally talented.

"Great," I said. "SRS's program has to work—if they don't get whatever information they need, I'm sure they'll find a way to blame me and that'll be the end of me going on missions."

"Got it!" Beatrix said excitedly. "I'll work on it tonight, and then tomorrow I'll get it—"

We both stopped. How could Beatrix get me the program before tomorrow morning? It wasn't like she could just send it to me in an envelope, and the HITS guys would definitely catch a rogue program if she tried to e-mail it. I'd have to get a hard copy from her tomorrow at the hospital. Otter would be able to spot a brush pass a mile away, so she'd have to drop it somewhere, somewhere only I would be able to pick it up. But I couldn't just root through a potted plant or in a light fixture with Otter standing right there . . .

"Are Ben and your uncle nearby?" I asked.

"Yep."

"Great. I'm going to need everyone's help with this."

CHAPTER FIFTEEN

Otter and I stepped into the elevator lobby at exactly eight o'clock. He gave me a bitter look, like he'd hoped I'd over-slept. We cut down a short hallway and emerged in a park-ing lot behind the substitute teaching school. There Otter unlocked a boxy-looking car with faded paint. I brushed some crumbs off the fabric seats before sitting down.

Otter turned on the radio to a truly terrible country sta-tion, and drove us out of Castlebury, toward Fairview. It wasn't until the city—complete with The League's tower—came into view that we spoke.

"So, I'm Clifton Harris, and the file said I live in south-ern Oregon," I said.

"That's right. And I'm your dad. Don't make that face—I don't like it any more than you do. The doctors will do your exam in a room with computers that require a fingerprint scan every time they wake up from sleep mode. So, when the doctor steps out of the room to go get your test results, I'll install the program. You just sit there, got it?" Otter said.

"Sure thing."

The children's hospital was an enormous building in the center of the city, just a few blocks over from The League's tower. It was mostly white, but windows on the top floors were decked out in red, yellow, and blue curtains, and there was a giant fountain with a teddy bear in the center in the front courtyard. Otter pulled into a parking spot, then stalled there while he shut his eyes, preparing for his character, I guessed. I checked my watch for the millionth time. This was going to be close—we were a little bit early.

"Let's go, Clifton." Otter turned the car off, pulled the parking brake, and then we both opened our doors. As Otter stepped out, he tapped the Lock button on the driver's side. The locks obediently popped down. As I went to shut my door, I quickly flipped mine back so the car was left unlocked.

Otter didn't notice.

I rubbed my temple and drooped my head in mock pain. When I reached the trunk of the car, Otter met me and put an arm around my shoulders, guiding his ill son toward the main hospital doors. When we crossed through them, the blast of cool air and the smell of flowers layered over antiseptic hit me. The lobby was decked out in paper butterflies and rainbow-colored rugs. This was the section for everyday illnesses, rather than superserious stuff, and you could tell—even the paper butterflies looked sort of bored.

"Slow down," I whined to Otter in what I hoped was a Clifton Harris voice. "It's freezing in here."

"That's just 'cause your temperature is so high. Here—take a seat and I'll sign us in," Otter said, ushering me over to a turquoise chair. My stomach clenched—were we early? We couldn't be early. I chanced lifting my eyes and glanced around the waiting room, then held in a sigh of relief. There were a few infants, some harried mothers with young children, and there, off to the side, were Clatterbuck and Ben.

Mission: Install dual spy programs without
Otter noticing, turning me in to SRS,
and putting me In the Weeds
Step 1: Ben and Clatterbuck get to the hospital first

I let my eyes graze over them, but I quickly looked back down at my hands when Ben grinned at me. I was sure he wasn't *trying* to blow my cover, but he was going to if he kept this up. I saw Clatterbuck elbow him through my peripheral vision. Ben's face crumpled and he went back to pretending to have a terrible stomach bug just as Otter finished with the sign-in sheet and rejoined me.

Step 1a: Ben gets called to go back first

"Benjamin Smith?" a voice called. I didn't look, but I heard Clatterbuck and Ben rise across the room. *Smith? Seriously, Clatterbuck? No, no, it'll work—it's so obvious, it's forgettable.* A door clicked shut, and now . . . I had to wait. Ben had one job, and no matter how small or easy it was, it was important. So much of this mission relied on everyone else doing their parts. As scary as it was, I think I preferred breaking into The League. At least there I had to rely on only myself.

"Clifton Harris?" the same voice called several minutes later. I let Otter spring up before me, then I rose slowly and dragged my feet behind him. The nurse who called my name smiled at me, then ushered me through the door.

I'd actually never been to a real hospital before. SRS had its own medical staff, of course, and they oversaw everything from allergies to knee-replacement surgery. I badly wanted to look around at the bustle of nurses and doctors, study the bulletin board of notes, and listen in on conversations in case I ever needed to replicate them someday for a disguise. The nurse brought me around a corner and took my weight, then measured my height, just like at SRS. And then, also like SRS . . .

"We'll need a urine sample, of course," she said brightly, like asking someone for pee was a happy thing.

"Right," I said, keeping my voice low and sickly. I plucked the plastic cup from her fingers.

Otter made small talk with the nurse while I stepped

into the little bathroom and shut the door, crossing my fingers that Ben hadn't been taken to some other bathroom after he'd been checked in. I hurried over to the toilet and very carefully took the lid off the back of the tank.

Step 2: Ben plants the flash drive in the bathroom

I grinned—there, floating in a sealed sandwich bag, was a chipped and ancient-looking purple flash drive. I fished it from the tank and pocketed the drive. It took me a few seconds more to fill the cup, and then I rejoined Otter in the hall. It was so seamless that I almost felt uneasy, like the bottom would fall out of the whole thing.

The nurse led Otter and me to a small exam room, the kind with paper bedding. Cartoon characters had been painted on the walls, and there, in the corner, was the computer, complete with fingerprint scanner. I took note that the USB ports were on the side of the monitor.

"Clifton!" a cheery voice said. A male doctor with red-and-gray speckled hair stepped in. He shook Otter's hand, then mine, and went through a dance of small talk while he pressed a stethoscope to my chest and asked me to take deep breaths. He looked in my eyes and my ears, listened while I told him I felt tired and my head hurt and how I hadn't missed any school yet, but worried I might, and I really couldn't because I wasn't getting a good grade in language arts. Not that it really mattered, since I wanted to be a music producer anyway.

Clifton Harris was a complex creature.

"Well, your results should be finishing up shortly—but I wouldn't worry too much," the doctor said, sliding onto a low stool and facing the computer. He pressed his finger against a reader; the computer obeyed, popping up a form for him to input new patient info. He typed up all my stats, and even made a note about how I wanted to be a music producer—for future doctor small talk times, I supposed. "Looks good! Give me just a moment, Clifton, to go grab your chart." He rose. I saw Otter's hand move toward his pocket, where the flash drive with SRS's program was.

Footsteps in the hall—heels, running, clacking loudly on the tile floor. The doctor lifted his eyebrows, and then he was nearly smacked in the face as the door to the exam room flung open. A wide-eyed nurse stood on the other side, pointing emphatically at Otter.

"Your car!" she said, panting, out of breath. "It's in the road!"

Step 3: Clatterbuck forces Otter to leave the room

"Huh?" Otter said.

"It's in the road—it rolled. It's in the intersection!" she said, stepping back.

I gritted my teeth in excitement. Clatterbuck had come through and done his part.

"Oh!" Otter's jaw locked, his eyes panicked. He looked from me to the doctor and back again and again.

"Go!" the doctor said swiftly. "Hurry!"

"I can't—Clifton—"

"I'll be fine, Dad, go!" I said urgently, biting my tongue when I finished, punishing myself for calling Otter "Dad." Otter gave me a mean look, but he didn't have a choice unless he wanted to totally blow our cover—what kind of man just lets his car sit in an intersection? He patted me on the shoulder swiftly and then took off down the hallway. I folded my arms over my chest nervously, catching the flash drive Otter had seamlessly tucked into my T-shirt collar before it fell all the way through to the floor. The doctor looked back at me.

"Wow! Well, let's hope everything goes fine with that. While he's saving the car, I'll go grab your results. Be back shortly!" He slipped out the door, closing it behind him.

Step 4: Install the programs

I leaped up and charged to the computer, nearly knocking the whole thing over as I slid onto the doctor's chair. I popped SRS's flash drive into the computer's USB port. I knew exactly how to install it—uploading spy software was something we'd learned in Kennedy's grade. I clicked through, tapping my foot anxiously. A caterpillar-green progress bar inched along painfully slowly. It finally loaded, and I typed frantically, making sure the program was deeply hidden inside the operating system. The relief I felt when everything was complete was short-lived. I yanked out Beatrix's bright purple flash drive and fumbled to push it into the USB. Nerves were getting to me—I took a deep breath.

Beatrix's program popped up, a white wall of text. I typed what she instructed me to yesterday: "beatrix is cooler than ben." The screen flashed for a moment, then it all went black and I felt the thick taste of panic rise in me. Something had gone wrong. We'd tripped a firewall, she'd accidentally wiped a system, the computer simply couldn't handle the program . . .

The screen returned. It looked normal—a chart with Clifton Harris's name on it.

"Huh," I said aloud, marveling at Beatrix's work. I heard a rustle outside, a step, a hand on the doorknob. I yanked the flash drive from the computer and dived onto the bed.

"Clifton! Good news!" the doctor said brightly, sweeping back into the room a millisecond after my butt hit the bed. "I think odds are that you've just got a bug. I've written you a prescription." The doctor paused to yank the top sheet off his pad. "Why don't you go back to the lobby to wait on your dad?"

When I got to the lobby, I fought the urge to laugh. No, wait, that was putting it too mildly—I fought the urge to fall on the floor, laughing and pointing like a cartoon character. Otter was standing in the middle of an intersection beside his boxy-shaped car, surrounded by cars with smashed bumpers and shattered headlights. Other drivers were shouting at him, hands on their hips and faces stretched in anger. Otter was yelling back, which wasn't helping. I suspected one woman was three seconds away from taking a swing.

It was perfect.

The hospital was focused on new patients now, so I slunk out the front door and hurried over to help him. Beatrix's purple flash drive made a pleasant *plunk* as I tossed it into the teddy bear fountain on my way to the intersection.

"Forget it, man—we're not letting you drive off. It's illegal not to have insurance in this state, you know!" an angry old man howled at Otter. He looked like the center of a rage-and-car-shaped flower.

"You're the one who hit my car!" Otter snapped back, livid. He was hanging on to the open driver's-side door, like it was holding him back from charging everyone down.

"You're the idiot who forgot to pull his parking brake! You're lucky the car didn't hurt someone when it rolled through the intersection!"

Otter stared at the car and made a combination of vowel sounds that were supposed to be words but hadn't quite cooked long enough in his brain. I could tell he was trying to remember if he'd pulled the parking brake or not. I, of course, knew he had—it was just that I'd left my door unlocked so that Clatterbuck could drop the brake and give the car a nice shove. I hadn't expected Clatterbuck to shove it quite *this* hard though. I figured the car would end up tapping the edge of the teddy bear fountain, or maybe denting a nearby car. Stopping traffic in the center of a major intersection? This was a little more than I'd bargained for when I set up the plan last night, and it was all starting to freak me out a little.

In the distance I heard the faint sound of police sirens. We had to get out of there before the cops came—because, from the twisted look on Otter's face, he didn't prepare false insurance or a false driver's license. Getting arrested wasn't rare for SRS members, but getting arrested for something like a traffic violation? That was just embarrassing. Plus, it would mean that no one would remember how successful our mission was—they'd just remember how big a mess had been made at the end of it. As much as the idea of Otter in handcuffs thrilled me, I had to get us out of here. I looked around, taking stock of what we could use, but there was nothing except a fallen bumper or two, some broken glass, and an ever-growing crowd of onlookers, staring like this was some sort of incredibly boring movie . . .

Movie.

That'll work.

"Whoa, wait—is that gasoline?" I said, frantically pointing to a pool of liquid underneath Otter's car. It wasn't gasoline—it was just windshield wiper fluid, if I was remembering Emergency Car Acquisition (or what we affectionately called Grand Theft Auto) class correctly. "It is! Dad, we've gotta get away! The whole thing might blow up!"

People's eyes widened, Otter's included. They looked at the gasoline and hurriedly backed up toward their cars like they weren't positive they believed me, but they'd seen plenty of car explosions in movies. And just like Ben back at The League, they all assumed that movies were correct. Otter suddenly realized what I was doing and ducked into the driver's seat and slammed the door. He unlocked the doors at the same moment he turned the key in the ignition; I'd barely shut my door before he peeled out of the intersection through the space the others had left when they slunk away from the potentially exploding car.

I was relieved. I expected Otter to be too, but he mostly looked shaken. I'd have felt bad for him, if I didn't dislike him so much.

"So, the program is installed. I had plenty of time. Everything should be good," I said curtly. I pulled the gray SRS flash drive from my pocket and dropped it in the cup holder unceremoniously.

"I must have not pulled the parking brake."

I didn't say anything.

He continued, voice blank, "It nearly messed up the whole mission. Do you know my mission success rate? It's perfect. Absolutely perfect."

"What about the Acapulco incident my dad mentioned?"

"That wasn't my fault. I didn't know the parrot could talk!" Otter finally exploded, sending spit all over the windshield. I shrunk back as he continued to mutter angrily to himself about parking brakes and parrots. It wasn't until we were well out of the city and nearly back to SRS headquarters that he calmed down. At a stoplight he turned to me.

"You're not to tell anyone about the incident with the parking brake."

"What? Why not? It's going in your mission report anyway—"

"Hale Jordan," he said, his voice dangerous. "You are not to tell anyone. Are we clear?"

I ran my tongue across my teeth. Otter was annoying, and he hated me, and he was entirely too sensitive about whatever happened in Acapulco, but he was still a dangerous man to cross. However, this was too perfect a chance to pass up. I shook my head.

"I'm not lying for you. You'd have told everyone at SRS if *I'd* been the one to screw up the whole thing."

For a second I was actually afraid Otter was going to punch me. Instead he gripped the steering wheel tighter, ignoring the fact that the light had changed. "Fine. I'll tell everyone there was a problem, and you had to install the program. Make you out to be a real hero. But no one hears that I forgot to pull the brake."

"Okay, that fixes half of it," I said, nodding. "Because I

saved your butt by installing the program. But I saved your butt *again* by creating a diversion so we could escape the intersection before the cops showed up. You owe me for that too."

Otter cursed—loudly. Several times, and in several languages. I could practically see the battle in his head: Which was worse? Admitting to everyone that Hale Jordan saved him? Or admitting to Hale Jordan that he owed him?

"Fine. What do you want for the second one?"

"I want to go on another mission."

"You're not a junior agent," he hissed. I shrugged, and he cursed several times in English. "Fine. I'll tell Director Fishburn that I think you should go on another mission. But that's the best I can do."

"Perfect."

CHAPTER SIXTEEN

Otter and I told Fishburn that he'd been called out of the room by the doctor to discuss something to do with my test results, which is why I had to install the program. It worked like a charm—Fishburn was delighted I'd come through. I guess everyone loves an underdog story.

"Kennedy!" I shouted as I walked into our apartment. I frowned when I saw the couch—Ms. Elma had been stabbing the upholstery again, then sewing it back together. Living with us wasn't very good for her head, which was worrisome. How much longer before they sent me and Kennedy to live in the SRS dorms? I shook off the concern. Once I got my parents back, living at SRS wasn't going to happen, period. Where would we live? A house somewhere? League headquarters?

My mind twisted—after everything that'd happened,

it was still hard to picture living anywhere but apartment 300. I headed toward my room to change into clothes that didn't smell like a hospital, reminding myself that when my parents came home, they'd sort out where we would live. "Kennedy, where are you? Want to hear about my mission?" I called for her again.

I walked to my bedroom and frowned. It sounded like my clock radio was on, turned up full blast. I creaked open my bedroom door. When it was just a few inches open, someone crashed into me. Kennedy—I could tell from the flash of red hair. She weighed so little that she didn't so much knock me to the ground as drag me there slowly.

"Hey, what—what are you doing?" I said, half laughing. I found her face in the sea of hair and neon green shorts. Her eyes were wide, and she was holding a finger to her lips frantically. I let her finish dragging me to the carpet and then leaned in so she could whisper in my ear.

"Someone bugged our apartment."

My heart sank deep into my stomach, dissolving among the bile that immediately twisted around in my gut. The apartment was bugged. Someone at SRS heard the conversation I'd had with The League last night. I was caught. There was no point in running—it was all over.

Kennedy jerked a finger toward my bed, and together we slowly, silently lifted the comforter up. On the bed, among my ruffled blankets, was the bug she'd discovered. A ruby earring and bracelet set.

"I turned on the radio real loud, so I don't think they can hear us now, but who knows how long they've been here? They're old—I don't think they're SRS, Hale. I think . . . I think . . ." She dropped her voice even lower so that I almost couldn't hear her at all. "I think The League planted them."

"Oh, no, I don't . . . I don't think it's The League," I said, trying to keep the visible relief off my face. "Maybe one of my friends planted it in here as a joke."

Kennedy's face twisted, and I could tell she knew this was a lie but didn't want to come right out and say, *But, Hale, you don't really have any friends anymore*. Instead she stared at the jewelry and clenched her small hands into fists.

"Well, if that's the case, I'm reporting them. They can't keep acting like this—"

"No! No, don't report it." I was torn between horror that she might report the bracelet, and humiliation that my little sister was now trying to stand up to bullies for me. This was a new level of lame.

Kennedy put her hands on her hips. I could tell she wanted to get much louder, perhaps even yell, but she didn't dare while stranger ears were listening. "Hale, they *bugged our house*. What if they *are* from The League, and this is how they got Mom and Dad?"

"Why were you going through the linen closet anyway?"

Kennedy gave me a sour look but then cracked. She ducked her head to the ground and seemed to shrink before my eyes. "I didn't want to go snooping around in Mom and Dad's room, since it smells like Ms. Elma now and that freaks me out. But the blankets in the closet still . . . They still smell like Mom, and so . . . wait." She froze. Then she lifted an eyebrow. "I never told you I found them in the linen closet."

I exhaled. *Well. Way to be a great spy, Hale. You just burned yourself to your little sister.*

"Come over here," I said. Kennedy and I walked to the bed. We sat down on the edge together, and I reached back to pick up the jewelry set. "You don't need to be afraid of these. I put them in the linen closet."

"*You* bugged our house?" Kennedy asked.

"No. I was hiding them in our house. I didn't want Ms. Elma to find them. I didn't want you to find them either, but I figured you would if I left them in my bedroom. So . . . don't freak out, but—you're right. These do belong to The League."

Her eyes widened. She was freaking out, but she was doing so silently, and I didn't admonish her for it. I continued.

"Kennedy, when I was in the League building, they told me that . . . Well . . ." I launched into the entire story—how SRS were the bad guys, how The League were helping me figure out Project Groundcover, how I was officially a double agent. I ended it all by showing her the printout of Mom and Dad's file, the one that showed them listed as In the Weeds.

I didn't think it was possible, but her eyes widened even

more. I poked her in the stomach, forcing her to breathe, which seemed to do her some good.

"Are you sure, Hale? Really, really sure? Because this is big. Like . . . huge," she whispered.

I nodded. "I'm positive. I wouldn't do it if I weren't positive. I think working with them might be the only way to get our parents back."

"In the Weeds. They listed The Team as In the Weeds," she said breathlessly. I thought she was about to cry, but then Kennedy reached over and picked up the jewelry from my hand. She somewhat shakily wrapped the bracelet on her wrist and clipped the earrings to her earlobes. She looked ridiculous—like a little girl playing dress-up with her grandmother's costume jewelry. She lifted the bracelet to her lips and whispered.

"Hello?"

"They might not answer if it's not me. They're underfunded, but I don't think they're going to just talk to any old person who comes across the com—"

"My name's Kennedy," she said, her voice warming a little. I put my head in my hands. *Seriously, Clatterbuck? What if she was someone from SRS looking to bust me?* "Yeah," she continued, now growing more enthusiastic. "That was me! Hale and I wrapped all those guys up in the sign? And I tied that girl up in a net trap? Oh! Yeah, I would like to talk to her—I felt a little bad about the whole thing. She seemed nice."

I tried to feel bad, tried to make my gut twist with guilt

for bringing Kennedy into all this insanity. But, as she kicked back on my bed and bicycled her legs absently at the ceiling, talking to Beatrix—or was it Ben on the other line now? I wasn't sure—I couldn't help but feel relieved that there was one less person to keep my secrets from.

"Kennedy, no. You can't come with me. If I get caught, I'm not taking you down with me," I said. Again. And again. And again. It was starting to sound like a song.

"You just never want me to do *anything*," Kennedy said. Or someone with Kennedy's voice said. It was a Disguise Day, and she'd been made up to be a brunette with zero freckles and thick eyebrows. She looked nothing like Kennedy, but she still bounced around like a deer that'd had too many sodas. I was halfway through applying my own disguise—a very old man with droopy eyes. It was a difficult one, and talking to Kennedy kept making the silicone wrinkles on my cheeks crack off. I reapplied a wrinkle and gave Kennedy a pointed look.

"What? It's not my fault you're becoming an old man. No one else picked one that hard," she said, nodding toward the rest of the SRS student body. All together there were about seventy-five of us, and we were spread out around the cafeteria. The Disguise Department, which was usually carefully tended to and cataloged by a handful of agents, appeared to have exploded on us—tables were *covered* in

wigs and makeup pots and spilled spirit gum bottles—
which was exactly why Disguise Days only came once every
few weeks. I watched a group of eight-year-olds being taught
how to put wigs on.

"Hale! Please!" Kennedy whined.

"No. It's too dangerous," I said, fixing one of my wrinkles
again.

"More dangerous than staying here with the people who
want our parents dead?" she asked, and I nearly tackled her
to quiet her down. She looked pleased to have my full attention now, and she dropped her voice to continue seriously.
"I'm going to take my junior agent exam soon, Hale, and
then I'm going to be a double agent like you. Because you're
my brother, and if something happens to you, I'll be stuck
here all alone."

I frowned, because this actually hadn't occurred to me.
Kennedy was *never* alone—she was almost always surrounded by friends—but she was right, of course. She'd be
all alone, and in the way that counted. I sighed. "But I also
can't just let you—"

"Let you what?" a male voice said behind me. I didn't
have to turn and look—I saw them reflected in my mirror.
Walter and the Foreheads. All three of them were wearing
padded suits underneath their standard SRS uniforms, and
they'd used silicone to plump up their cheeks.

They'd disguised themselves as me. Well—a hilarious,

super-fat, super-geeky version of me. Their eyes glowed, and they cracked up when they saw the look of recognition on my face.

"You like them? We used all the padding they set out," Walter said. How could this possibly be the same guy who told me he was sorry about my parents just a few days ago? It was like he'd gotten eaten by jerk aliens.

"Love them," I said. "You look like someone who might do an amazing job improvising on a mission. Maybe someone that Fishburn would make a special announcement about?"

After the hospital mission for Evergreen, Fishburn had made a point of coming to my class to tell everyone what a great job I'd done improvising, and how I'd really saved the day. Otter repeated the sentiments, though he didn't appear happy about having to call me "the hero of the day." Fishburn *never* came to classrooms, so there was a lot of speculation as to why our mission warranted a visit. I heard everything from "Hale actually took a bullet for Otter, but we're not supposed to know" down to "Fishburn just wanted to make Hale feel good, since his parents are missing."

No matter what the theory, no one debated whether or not I'd done an excellent job. It didn't make me popular or faster or a junior agent, but it did make me a lot better armed for conversations like this one.

"We look like *losers*," Cameron corrected me.

"So I see," I said.

"Because we're dressed as you!" Cameron added, growing frustrated that I still didn't appear offended. "Get it? Because we're fat—"

"Just shut up," Walter said, shoving Cameron. I wondered if SRS had a specialty program for people who would make especially good doorstops. Cameron seemed like a contender for a spot.

"Yeah," Kennedy said, putting her hands on her hips. "All of you shut up. Hale is twenty times the spy you are."

Walter laughed hard. "He's twenty times the spy we are, that's for sure," he said, grabbing his fake stomach. Kennedy looked wounded; I gave her a weary look and she trudged back to join her classmates, clearly more embarrassed than I was about the whole thing. I glued another piece of silicone on, ignoring Walter and the Foreheads, who looked disappointed with the short lifespan of their joke.

"Hale," someone said in a gravelly voice. Walter and the Foreheads stepped away to reveal Ms. Elma and Otter, though I wasn't totally sure which one had said my name. Ms. Elma's scar made the plastic ones the ten-year-olds were applying look ridiculous.

"I need some measurements," she said. "Disguise for your next mission."

Jaws dropped. I went ahead and dropped mine, too, because even though I wasn't surprised, given how good my dirt on Otter was, I needed to look it.

"He's going on another mission?" Walter asked, voice cracking. "But he hasn't even tested into junior agent yet!"

"It was Fishburn's decision," Otter said immediately, which I know was supposed to mean *I didn't do this*. He still couldn't look me in the eyes. I was pretty okay with that.

Ms. Elma was flickering around, her tape measure whipping me like a lizard's tongue. She scribbled some information onto a pad and then turned to Walter. "You too."

"What? I'm going on another mission?" Walter grinned but then realized what this meant. "Wait—I'm going on a mission with *him*?"

"Stop fidgeting," Ms. Elma said, oblivious to Walter's social concerns. She wrapped the tape measure around Walter's head as he looked pleadingly at Otter.

The Foreheads were laughing so hard that the padding in their Hale costumes was jiggling out.

"Please. Come on, man. Don't send me with him. Call it a favor. I'll clean your office. I'll take venom-collecting duty for a week."

"I don't assign missions, Quaddlebaum," Otter said, and then turned to walk away. He called back over his shoulder, "It's Operation Evergreen, just like your last mission, Jordan. Briefing files will be delivered tonight." I saw a sort of pleased sneer on his face, which was never a good sign. Anytime Otter was pleased, I was miserable.

CHAPTER SEVENTEEN

Kennedy won. I was taking her to The League.

She'd used a tried-and-true method of younger siblings everywhere: she'd begged and begged until I would rather have removed my own eyeballs than listen to her beg anymore. Plus, I was worried that if I didn't take her, eventually someone *else* would hear her begging, and we'd be in a real disaster. Since Kennedy didn't have an errand-running excuse to leave, and even I was concerned about drawing too much attention with dry-cleaning runs, we crept out through the garage.

"What did you tell Ms. Elma?" I asked her as we rushed past rows and rows of solid black bulletproof sedans, flashy convertibles, and more well-armored SUVs than I could count.

"That I'm hanging out with Ridley and Emily."

"And if she asks Ridley's and Emily's parents?"

Kennedy gave me an exasperated look. "Emily's in the dorms, and I bet whoever is playing dorm parent for the weekend won't know the difference. And Ridley's mom will assume I *am* with Ridley, who is spending the weekend with Emily and Jordan—"

"Okay, okay, I just wanted to make sure."

"I know how to build a cover story, Hale. I got the highest grade in my Emergency Undercover Ops class last year, remember?"

"Still not as high as my score in it was," I said, elbowing her by way of apology. She gave me an even more exasperated look and then grinned.

"So what did *you* tell Ms. Elma?" she asked.

"That I was going to the library to practice my Arabic."

"That's it? Studying in the library?"

"It's where I go every weekend, almost," I said as we cut through a side door and emerged on the back side of the substitute teacher school, where the less fancy cars— like the one Otter and I took to the children's hospital— sat in the parking lot. The fact that I really did spend most weekends studying made my story both pathetic and believable.

"Hale," someone cough-said as we approached the fancy toy store—today's meeting point. It was Clatterbuck, wearing a truly terrible fake beard and three different types of plaid. He was also still wearing his emerald com unit. I glanced around to double-check for any roaming SRS agents and, seeing none, guided Kennedy toward him.

"Kennedy!" Clatterbuck said, clapping her on the shoulder. He was making his voice all round, like he was trying to be Santa.

"Why are you dressed like a crazy person?" Kennedy asked, though she was grinning.

"I'm not—I'm a logger! See!" Clatterbuck jerked his thumb over his shoulder. There was, indeed, a log truck idling in back of the parking lot. "You said I should use different cars when I pick you up, Hale, remember? No one will ever think a logger is an agent!" Clatterbuck was giddy, and every time he waggled his eyebrows enthusiastically, his fake beard shifted a little off-center. He pointed at Kennedy's owl-sticker-covered shoes. "Hey—I like those!"

"Thanks! I like your earrings—I mean, com unit," Kennedy answered, beaming.

Clatterbuck drove us back to The League in the log truck, which smelled like sap and cigarettes and was full of pine needles. Kennedy very literally sat on the edge of her seat the entire time, fingertips clutching the windowsill in some combination of excitement and fear. Clatterbuck noticed, and offered her some maple candy that he'd found in the glove compartment. It was super sticky, so trying to chew it occupied her for most of the remaining trip.

At League headquarters, Kennedy, Clatterbuck, and I

joined Oleander, Beatrix, and Ben in the tiny cafeteria. Oleander had ordered another pizza, which we destroyed quickly as we discussed the hospital mission. Kennedy was mostly listening, like she was afraid that if she spoke and made her presence known, she'd be thrown out entirely.

"Well, Beatrix," Oleander said, overenunciating her name. Oleander hadn't said it outright, but it was clear she was a little uncomfortable with just how many kids were involved in her spy organization these days. "Has anything come of watching SRS's hospital program?"

Beatrix adjusted her glasses and then removed her Right Hand from her backpack. "Kind of. Maybe it'll make sense to you, Hale. SRS isn't really *doing* anything with the hospital's computers. They're just watching them."

"Huh? Why do they want to watch a children's hospital?" I asked.

"I have no idea. I figured there must be some super-secret pharmaceutical something that they wanted. But all they're doing is looking at records. You know—heights. Weights. Names. Yesterday someone named their baby Sparkle, by the way. Sparkle Star Nelfman."

"I *love* it!" Kennedy said brightly. All eyes turned to her. She clapped a hand over her mouth, and then removed it to mutter, "I mean, I like the Sparkle Star part."

"They're going back through everyone who was born in the last fifteen years or so, and it looks like they're flagging files where the doctor has written extra stuff about school or accomplishments or things," Beatrix continued.

"Interesting," Oleander said, frowning till her eyebrows nearly touched. "Maybe they're searching for a specific baby? Someone very important—a diplomat's or tycoon's kid? Maybe someone they could hold for ransom . . . I suppose even SRS can always use some extra money, and something small like Operation Evergreen sounds like a way they'd scheme up to get it. Doesn't get us any closer to Groundcover, though, and that's what's most important. Beatrix, I don't suppose you can use their program to trace your way back and hack into SRS itself?"

Beatrix groaned. "Trust me, I tried. But they basically have their own little island on the Internet. There's no way in because their main system doesn't connect to anything else. If I were *inside* SRS, sure, I could hack it. But from out here? Sorry."

"All right, all right," Oleander said, putting a hand to her temple to think of something else. "Then, Hale, the upcoming mission you're assigned to—is it Groundcover?"

"No. It's another mission for Operation Evergreen. By the way—I remembered you guys mentioning someone named Creevy the first time I was here. He's assigned to Groundcover, just like my parents."

Clatterbuck made a grumbly noise under his breath. "Figures he'd be assigned to it. Creevy was an SRS agent back in my day. We knew he was an important asset, and we knew he was involved with some pretty major missions, but we could never figure out who he was, what he looked like, how old he was . . . nothing. He was dangerous. Took out some of our best agents . . ." He drifted off and looked sad, which was a strange expression to see on Clatterbuck's face.

Oleander pressed her lips together. "Well, just one more reason we need to make Groundcover the goal. We'll figure this out." She paused. "Hale."

"Come to the gym," Ben said when Oleander and Clatterbuck left. "I've been working on some inventions for your next mission."

"Really? Thanks," I said, feeling rather proud. I mean, back at SRS, I couldn't get anyone to take me seriously. Here at The League? I was suddenly the top agent, with someone creating new devices just for me. After being Fail Hale for so long, it felt almost disorienting to be the star.

"He doesn't even know what his next mission is yet," Kennedy pointed out as we trundled down the steps and into the basement. Kennedy wrinkled her nose up at the room's smell.

"That's why I pretty much covered all the basics," Ben said, looking pleased. He walked to the center of the room and whisked away a sheet from a large table, revealing what at first looked like a pile of abandoned junk, but on closer inspection was actually a pile of inventions.

"Whoa," Kennedy said. "What's this—"

"Oh, be careful! That's the BENchwarmer. It extends and becomes sort of like a battering ram, I guess. Sometimes it explodes, though."

Kennedy gently placed the BENchwarmer back on the table, looking very impressed.

Ben took us through a few of the others. The CaBEN, which was a weird little pop-up tent that zipped to the size of your palm. The DustBEN, which he unfortunately demonstrated—it created an enormous dust cloud that was supposed to help you escape, but mostly just made us cough. Kennedy's favorite was the CariBENer, which was a pretty cool gadget that fit inside a backpack but hooked into the cabling of bridges so you could creep along underneath them (Kennedy wanted to try it, but Ben said it was still in testing). Then there was the BEN Seeing You.

"It delivers a pulse that knocks someone out—you just hold that end down against skin, pull the trigger, and boom, they're out!" Ben explained. "I made it from pipe cleaners and lasers. Anyway, here—I put some of them on this utility belt for you, like the one Uncle Stan says he used to carry." Ben revealed a somewhat patchwork belt that had a half dozen pockets and compartments on it. He began tucking the finished devices into it—they fit perfectly. I didn't know exactly where I'd use something like the CaBEN, but I had to admit, it was a cool thing to have. I went to snap it on.

"Aw, man, it's too small," Ben said when the belt stopped about two inches from closing.

I tensed—at SRS, this would be prime Hale the Whale time.

"Sorry, Hale. I'll fix it though. Oh, I know! I've been working on these new hooks that snap automatically!"

"Those keep cutting off your circulation," Beatrix reminded him absently from where she sat, staring at her Right Hand.

Ben shrugged at me.

"Thanks for making this, Ben. It's okay, though, that it doesn't fit. I mean, I can't really wear a League belt when I'm on a mission for SRS, you know?"

"Right," Ben said, but his face fell in a way that told me he'd forgotten this in the excitement of inventing all the gadgets to put on the belt.

"How about I just take it anyway, though, and that way I've got a good way to store all your inventions, even if I can't wear the belt," I offered, and Ben seemed satisfied with this compromise.

"Huh," Beatrix suddenly said. We all turned to look at her. She had her Right Hand out and was frowning at it. "Ben, they just got to our birth records. SRS, I mean. They're downloading them now."

"You were born in that hospital?" I asked.

"Yep, but actually, it doesn't matter—that hospital's computers network with a whole bunch of other hospitals, so they're pulling records from all over the place. I mean, it's not like they were looking for Ben and me specifically. They're downloading tons—I just happened to see our names go by."

"So what does that mean?" Kennedy asked. I turned to see that she was doing back walkovers down one of the gym's mats, which was comforting. I mean, I figure you only do walkovers when you feel pretty at ease in a place.

"It means—wow, you're flexible—it means nothing," Beatrix said. "Just interesting, that's all. Let's not tell Uncle Stan, though, okay, Ben? He'll just worry."

"Where are your parents?" Kennedy said. The question dropped on us like a heavy weight, and I felt stupid for not telling Kennedy what little I knew about Beatrix and Ben's parents ahead of time, just to avoid this situation.

Ben glanced at Beatrix before responding. "They were League agents," he said, and his voice had a slowness to it I hadn't heard before. It was a slowness I was familiar with, one that I'd heard other kids at SRS use when their parents didn't return from missions. It said: *They were agents, and they were killed in the field.* Hearing it from Clatterbuck was one thing, but hearing it from Ben's mouth was quite another.

I didn't know what to say, but thankfully Kennedy did. She gave them a kind of half smile, and said, "Our parents are agents too." It was totally unnecessary she tell them that, of course—because they knew, and Kennedy knew they knew, and yet all the same suddenly I realized that even though Ben and Beatrix weren't technically spies, the four of us weren't really so different from one another after all. I still didn't like group projects, but if I had to choose a team to work with, I'd choose the two of them and Kennedy over the SRS junior agents any day of the week.

Even if not a single one of us had passed the stupid junior agent exam.

A few hours later—after Kennedy tried, in vain, to teach Beatrix a cheer and Ben accidentally set off three firecrackers attempting to make some sort of flash-bang device inside a cupcake—Clatterbuck drove Kennedy and me back to SRS in his log truck. He'd removed the logs, somehow, in the past few hours, because "It wouldn't make sense for me to return with logs. That's not how loggers work." We went around the substitute teaching college and back through the garage. Ms. Elma lifted her head when we walked in the door, her pencil-thin eyebrows rising so high into her hairline that they almost disappeared entirely.

"Hale, finally," Ms. Elma said, getting up. "You've been gone all day."

"Arabic's a big language," I answered, but Ms. Elma wasn't listening to me anyhow.

She walked to the kitchen counter that, were our parents here, would have been covered in dishes, but had now been perfectly cleaned and wiped down for far too long. I couldn't believe I legitimately missed dirty dishes. There was a thick folder and a pile of fabric on the counter, both of which she lifted. "This is your uniform for the mission tomorrow. And Agent Otter dropped off this file for you to study." She shoved Otter's folder into my hands and then carefully draped the uniform over my free arm. I frowned and looked down at the file. On the front was typed:

Operation Evergreen
[Hale Jordan]
[Cover: Quincy Delfino]

"Quincy," I said. "What's the uniform?"

"Genius, is what it is," Ms. Elma said over her shoulder as she sat back down at the kitchen table. "Pure genius."

Pure genius was, more specifically, a baseball uniform. I didn't see the brilliance in it until I put it on in my bedroom, where I realized Ms. Elma had indeed done a genius job of tailoring it to fit me perfectly. If Walter had the same one, I was sure he looked better in it, but I had to admit that there were way more embarrassing things I could be wearing—like the actual SRS uniform, for example. As it was, I looked sort of like the stocky baseball player—maybe a catcher or a pitcher, someone who didn't usually have to run that far. I lifted the folder and opened it up to see what in the world I was doing that would involve a disguise like this, and groaned.

Welcome to Nelson Sports Academy
Where Pain Is Weakness Leaving the Body

CHAPTER EIGHTEEN

Nelson Sports Academy was a series of white warehouse gymnasiums connected via covered walkways. There were giant banners hanging off the sides that depicted silhouettes of kids running, dunking baskets, leaping over hurdles, and backflipping on balance beams. And, in giant red letters across the door, was that same slogan about weakness leaving the body.

Basically, Nelson Sports Academy was the worst.

Especially since I had to spend the day there with Walter, looking for an opportunity to sneak into the main office and steal a long list of student files from the owner's desk drawer for Operation Evergreen. I couldn't work out why SRS wanted files on a bunch of kids from a sports academy anyway—were they finally creating Kennedy's SRS cheerleading squad? Or maybe Oleander was right—maybe they were looking to kidnap a specific kid and hold him for some kind of ransom. I tried to ignore the queasy feeling in my stomach over that prospect.

In addition to baseball uniforms, Walter and I had been given some registration paperwork and two sack lunches to complete our disguises as new recruits. I'd managed to hide the too-small utility belt Ben had given me and my League com unit underneath the peanut-butter-and-ketchup sandwich Ms. Elma had made (she'd insisted that tomatoes were a fruit, so it was a legitimate peanut-butter-and-jelly sandwich, but I definitely wasn't going to eat it). The plan was for Clatterbuck and the others to listen in on the mission via the com and, if possible, I would relay some of the file information back to them so we could figure out what SRS was up to.

"We're here," Walter said breathlessly as we pulled up in a minivan—it was meant to make it look like we were being dropped off by our mom. I took the time to go over my legend again. Quincy Delfino. From Long Island. Parents are real estate investors. Varsity baseball player. I turned the facts over and over in my head. I could do this. So long, of course, as they didn't *actually* expect me to play baseball.

The agent who was playing our mom turned around in her seat. She lifted our brown bag lunches—my heart stopped for a second, thinking about how close she was to The League's stuff—and shoved them in our direction. Both of us had been given pocket digital scanners so we could make copies of the files SRS wanted. I wondered if Walter's was in his lunch bag, like mine was, or taped on his leg somewhere.

"Have a good first day!" she said loudly. Then, quietly, and with far less enthusiasm, "I'll return for you at fifteen hundred hours."

We got out of the car and faced the building as the agent drove away. Like most of SRS's work, this was a "clean mission," which meant that we were supposed to get in and out without anyone ever realizing a spy organization had been creeping around. The only way that would work was if the agent—our mom—left and then came to pick us up when school was over, like any other parent would. Walter, who looked unsurprisingly fantastic in his baseball uniform, hurried to the main doors. He paused.

"I'm Nathan Delfino. Third baseman. Two Little League World Series wins," he whispered to himself. His voice was jumpy—not scared, exactly, but punchy in a way that didn't fit with all the bragging he'd done about his first field mission, back at that chess championship. I frowned at him. Plenty of seemingly perfect agents had trouble pulling it together in the field—and given his voice and the jitter in his step, it looked like Walter might be one of them. I stepped forward and opened the door, since I was beginning to doubt Walter had the nerve to do it.

Step 1: Enroll at Nelson Sports Academy

This place looked like some sort of Olympic facility. There were timers along the walls, mats on the floors, people tumbling past us again and again and again while heavyset coaches shouted at them in foreign languages. There were signs in the little lobby area, pointing us to other gyms for wrestling, basketball—even ballet. Another sign told us the main office was down the hall to our right. When we arrived, I saw the door held a list of junior Olympians and a sign-up sheet for a twenty-four-hour endurance run, which wasn't something I even knew existed.

"New students?" said an old man with a cactus-like beard when we pushed the main office door open. The place was clean and looked well organized, but the smell of plastic gear and foot powder was overwhelming despite the efforts of a coffeemaker hissing away in the corner. There were rows and rows of thick file cabinets behind a large desk, and opposite that, a wall of cubbies that appeared to be full of students' cell phones, purses, and street clothes. I could hear the muffled sound of piano music coming through the wall—I guessed the ballet studio? The coach rolled his eyes as the music swelled. "Wouldn't kill them to dance to something with a groove," he muttered, and then walked over to the file cabinets. "Your names?"

"Nathan and Quincy Delfino," Walter said a little too quickly. "Baseball, sir."

"I'm not *sir*—I'm *Coach*," the man said. "Forms, please." We handed them over. Coach scanned through them.

"Little League World Series. Nice. Now, look—just because your father owns most of Montana and a good portion of Texas doesn't mean you're going to get special treatment here. You want to be pampered? Go to Wellington Sports Prep with the other sissies. You think we give the Prime Minister of Brunei's son special treatment? No. He's doing laps with the rest of them. And speaking of laps, you're gonna get them today for being late, I'm sure."

"On the first day?" I said, pouting. I figured Quincy Delfino was sort of a whiner. Coach rolled his eyes at me, and then dropped Walter's and my forms into folders, which he turned and put into the file cabinet behind him.

"All right, rookies. Baseball practices on the fields. Go through these doors, down the stairs, past the wrestling gym, around the side, and you'll see them. You can't miss them."

"Thanks. Hey, when's lunch, by the way?" I asked.

Coach gave me a long, appraising look. "Wouldn't hurt you to think of something other than food, son. Lunch is at noon—most of the other students buy theirs here, since we've specially formulated meals for peak performance. For today just leave your bags in the cubbies," he said, jerking his hand toward the wall. I was a little wary to leave all my League stuff—and SRS's pocket scanner—in a random cubby. Walter looked horrified at the prospect, but neither of us really had much of a choice, since Coach was watching. We shoved our lunch bags into a cubby together and then left the main office. Walter immediately started toward the baseball fields, just like Coach had instructed.

"Stop," I hissed. "What are you doing?"

"Our mission—there's a plan, Hale, and we have to follow it. Though I understand if you'd rather wait here for lunch," Walter snapped.

"Don't be stupid—I was asking so I could find out when Coach would be out of the office."

Step 2: Sneak out of baseball practice and collect the files

Walter's face fell. It took a lot of willpower for me not to look smug.

"Anyway—we can't go to the baseball fields. They're on the other side of the world. We'll never be able to get back here to collect the files," I continued.

Walter's eyes flitted from one end of the hall to the other. "But . . . that was the plan . . ."

I gave him an impatient look. "We'll have to pick another sport—something closer to the office." I looked down at my baseball uniform. "I guess we can't exactly go to gymnastics dressed like this."

Walter nodded, like the very act of creating a new plan would help his nerves. "Maybe we could pass the pants off as . . . Hm. What do soccer players wear?" Walter asked as he untucked his shirt, trying out a few variations on the baseball uniform. Eventually he took it off entirely, revealing his sleek black SRS uniform underneath.

"Oh. Oh, no. No, no, that can't be the only way," I groaned, putting my head into my hands.

"What? What's the way?" Walter asked, stooping to try to turn his baseball pants into something soccerlike.

I exhaled and pointed through the closest window. The ballet students were lined up at the barre, and piano music rose and fell like waves around them as they bent knees, extended toes, and tilted chins up like they found the hardwood floors too good for them. There were mostly girls, but a handful of boys, and every single one of them was wearing a black leotard.

Step 2: Sneak out of ~~baseball~~ ballet class
and collect the files

"Oh!" Walter said when he saw what I meant. *"Oh."*

"Ballet is right by the main office. Look—we'd be able to see in the mirror when Coach leaves, even. Come on," I grumbled, and stripped my baseball shirt off. Walter looked like he had half a dozen Hale-in-his-uniform jokes on hand, but I guess none of them were as funny without the Foreheads around. I balled up my baseball uniform and chucked it into the nearest trash can. Walter followed suit.

"All right," I said. "I'll give you a cue, understand?"

"A cue? What do you mean? Tell me exactly," Walter said,

swallowing warily. I opened my mouth to explain my whole plan to him in detail—since, apparently, despite being a junior agent, Walter couldn't handle a little improvising—but suddenly the door to the ballet studio flung open.

"What are you doing out here? You should be in class!" the ballet mistress snapped. She was a tiny, troll-like woman, and she held a yardstick in one hand. I thought she and Ms. Elma would probably get along well.

"Sorry, ma'am—we're in your class, actually. New students," I said quickly, and then moved forward. I had to turn around to grab Walter's arm—he seemed suddenly paralyzed. We followed the ballet mistress into the room, and the entire class turned to face us like our entrance was choreographed. They looked sleek, put together, and quite a lot like clones.

"I was not told to expect new students," the ballet mistress said. She had a French accent, but it was so diluted that it was nearly undetectable. She grew closer, and I could see fire in her beady eyes. I considered what it would look like if she and Agent Otter got in a staring contest, then realized her comment about not having new students had been hanging in the air for quite some time.

"You didn't?" I frowned. "We're from Le Ballet de Quebec. I'm sorry you didn't receive word we were coming. I get the impression Nelson Academy doesn't value its ballet program very much. Coach said he hadn't finished our paperwork because he was busy dealing with the *sports*."

"He said *that*? That man. Baseball and football all the time. No respect for the ballet!" She rapped her yardstick on the nearest barre, and the crack echoed up into the ceiling and made the dancers jump. Still muttering about Coach, the ballet mistress finally pointed to a spot on the barre in the back of the room; Walter and I hustled to take our places there beside the male dancers.

The ballet mistress cued the music, and the pianist—a real pianist, I realized—launched into a fast and chirpy number. "Tendu combination!" the ballet mistress shouted.

I matched my feet to the dancers'. Or at least, I tried to. They moved so fast. First their feet were a V shape, then shoulder-width apart, and then they bent their knees and turned and began again and really, I began to think that SRS should consider investing in a ballet program. It would probably help agents learn to multitask. Walter was doing much better than I was, because of course he was. His toes weren't pointed and he wasn't exactly graceful, but at least his feet were moving in time. The ballet mistress circled around the class, eyeing everyone hawkishly. When she got to Walter, her nose crinkled. When she got to me, her entire face crinkled.

"To the floor!" she said, and the class spread out around the room, away from the barre. "Step, pas de bourrée, glissade, assemblé, right and left, repeat every eight counts!" The music began again, and the first row did the combination, then the second, then the third, our turn. I elected not to look in the mirror at my attempt, which was a mistake, because all I could see was Walter soaring like some sort of ballet prodigy. I was so busy being annoyed that I almost missed the main office door opening, and Coach walking out. I coughed a bit under my breath as the next exercise started again, and Walter met my eyes in the mirror. It was time.

This combination involved some sort of crazy, prancing jump. We stepped, chassé-ed, jumped up, and—

Bam.

I hit the ground like a rock, crumpling over myself and rolling a few steps. The piano music abruptly stopped, and everyone whirled around to face me, hands clasped to mouths.

Step 2. ~~Sneak~~ I get everyone's attention,
and Walter sneaks out of ~~baseball~~ ballet class
and collects the files

"I'm fine! I'm fine!" I struggled to stand, wincing in fake pain as I tried to put weight on my ankle.

"Drag him off to the side," the ballet mistress instructed.

"No, I want . . . I *need* to dance. This is just weakness leaving my body!" I protested as Walter swooped in to help me. I let my feet get tangled up in his legs, and I smacked against the ground again. I was finally able to give Walter a meaningful look. *Go!*

Finally Walter understood.

"I'll go get ice," Walter volunteered immediately.

"Ugh, fine, fine. I'll page the nurse. Everyone else take a water break or something. It was terrible anyhow," the ballet mistress said, and stalked toward the side door. I saw her pull a pack of long fancy cigarettes from her pocket, and a whoosh of misty air swept into the room when she opened the door, leaving it propped with her yardstick. Walter vanished into the hallway.

I rubbed my "hurt" ankle tenderly until the nurse arrived, pushing a wheelchair. I heaved myself into the chair piteously, and the other dancers gave me friendly looks as I left, which I thought was awfully nice of them given a) how long they'd known me and b) what a mockery I'd just made of their sport. I moaned in pain as the nurse pushed me along the hall. Walter should be in the office now; I began to groan a little louder while we passed it, both so he knew I was gone and to cover up any noise he might be making inside.

"I've just got to grab your file. I can't give you any medication without checking it for allergies," the nurse said, suddenly stopping my chair.

"I don't have any allergies!" I protested. I imagined Walter inside, in the middle of a dozen folders, caught red-handed. It would be my fault. Playing the support side on a mission was scarier than I'd thought—I didn't much like having someone else's success in my hands, especially since Walter's success seemed a little fragile to begin with. Did Clatterbuck feel this way back at the children's hospital?

"Quincy, please," the nurse said. "I promise, I'll be quick. Your last name was Delfino, right?"

"Right, but—" I was cut off as the nurse turned the knob and cracked the door open, her eyes still on me. Walter wasn't anywhere to be seen inside, which should have made me relax, but instead it made me even more nervous. Why wasn't he there already? What was the point in me playing support if he wasn't going to get the files?

"I'll hurry!" the nurse promised, and pushed the door the rest of the way open. I suddenly saw Walter—he was pressed up behind the door so that it shielded him from her view. He had at least eight folders in one hand, and the scanner SRS gave us to copy them in his right. Assuming he'd already scanned those eight, he still had . . . thirty-four to go. I nodded at him almost imperceptibly—I could buy him time to do the remaining thirty-four.

Step 2. ~~Sneak I get everyone's attention, and Walter sneaks out of baseball ballet class and collects the files~~ Improvise

"Owwwwww! I think it's swelling!" I shouted. The nurse rolled her eyes a little, but she had my folder in hand. She hurried to the door and looked down at my ankle, which clearly wasn't swelling. She gave me a curious look and then tilted my folder open. Suddenly her face changed; she closed the folder and gave me a tight sort of smile.

"You know, I need to check on something with Coach really quickly. Wait here for me?" she said.

"Wait? I can't walk! I should never have signed up for ballet. I should have—"

"Wait here," the nurse repeated, and hurried down the hall, her low heels tapping against the floor. I balled my hands into fists. She must have seen in my folder that I was supposed to be in baseball, not ballet. I should have told her that I hated baseball, that I loved ballet, that my father wasn't supportive of my need to pas de chat. I should have told her a thousand distracting stories that would have bought Walter more time.

But I hadn't acted fast enough. I slammed my hands against the arms of the wheelchair, furious with myself, and jumped to my feet. And Walter leaped straight up in the air when I slammed the office door open.

"Hale—*Quincy!* What—"

"She knows something's up. Let's move," I said sternly. "Where are you?"

"I've got the first twelve scanned in," he said, flinging a cabinet open. He began to fumble as our plan disintegrated.

"I'll work from the bottom up. Don't scan—we'll have to take the originals," I said, snatching my lunch bag from the cubby. I yanked out SRS's scanner and went to work on Zooblish, Undermeyer, Quailer, and Quigley, stacking the finished folders up on the desk behind me. *Move, move, move,* my mind chanted over and over as I rushed through five more names.

"They're coming," Walter said, and he was right. I could hear the nurse's heels on the floor again, but this time there were others with her.

"Let's take what we have," I said. "Come on." We burst through the office door.

And froze.

Blocking the exit was the nurse. And Coach. And, from the looks of it, the entire Nelson Sports Academy wrestling class.

CHAPTER NINETEEN

One of the wrestlers reached up and shoved a mouth guard past his lips, and then cracked his knuckles. They all looked both very unhappy and very strong.

"Well!" Coach said. *"Well!"*

I said nothing. Walter's hands trembled, but he did a decent job of trying to hide it.

"You think I'm *surprised* to see you here? You think I don't know what you're doing? I know *exactly* what you're doing."

"Oh yeah? What?" I asked. Keep them talking. As long as they're talking, they're not pummeling us.

"You're spies!" he snapped.

"Oh." I mean, I hated to be impressed, but this was the first time I'd heard of a target just guessing it outright.

"You're spies for Wellington Sports Prep!" Coach continued.

"Ooooooh," I said, nodding. This made more sense.

"You think you can steal my students' information? Think you can steal my students from me? Wellington is a joke! They don't even give out pushups there!" He turned to the wrestlers. "Get 'em, boys!"

The wrestlers lunged. Walter and I leaped backward and ran, folders flying, feet sliding on the tile floors. We burst through the ballet room and made for the exterior door the ballet mistress had used earlier. Walter sailed ahead, legs carrying him twice as far as me. The dancers watched, baffled, as he streaked out the door. I was right behind, right behind . . .

Then someone tackled me.

I hit the ground—again—with a loud *slap*, and this time I didn't need to pretend I was in pain. The weight of a half dozen wrestlers compounded on top of me, and before I could even imagine fighting them off, they had my arms twisted behind my back and my head pinned to the floor. The dancers were screaming, the ballet mistress was lighting a cigarette right at the front of the room, and Coach was cackling like he'd caught a brag-worthy fish rather than a twelve-year-old in spandex. They hauled me to standing and, military style, marched me back to the main office. They sat me down in the chair and, I suppose as an extra precaution, stuck my torso to it with athletic tape.

The wrestlers stepped back, pleased with their handiwork. "Miss Valerie, tell everyone to gather in the basketball gym—I don't want any risk of that boy who escaped sneaking back in and *polluting* our students with this Wellington talk," Coach said, and the nurse bounded off to obey. Sometime amid me getting taped to my seat, a wrestler had collected all my fallen folders and handed the bent-up pile of papers to Coach. I glanced over at the cubbies. There was my lunch bag, and in it, Ben's utility belt. Surely, there was something on the belt that could get me out of this—but I'd have to get to it first.

"So," Coach said. "This is revenge, huh? I take a few of your students, and suddenly you guys are sending over people to sneak into my baseball program. Should've realized you're not a baseball player." He paused, looking me up and down. "What sport *do* you play?"

"I'm really more of a team manager," I said dryly. Coach snorted and kept talking, but I ignored him. The wrestlers were standing on all sides of me, leaning against file cabinets or hanging out in the doorframe, like Coach's own personal wolf pack.

"Look," I said. "How about rather than you tie me up like this, I give you some information on Wellington?"

"Why would I want information on Wellington?"

"Why would *you* have sent spies to Wellington if you didn't?" I asked.

This was a gamble, but I figured that the only reason Coach would be so quick to assume Walter and I were

Wellington spies was because the idea hit a little too close to home. Coach frowned, and for a moment I thought I'd misjudged him. But then he gave a crazed sort of grin.

"All right, all right. How about, for each thing you tell me about Wellington, I'll loosen a little of that tape? Give me excellent information—like, say, who they plan on putting forward for the Olympic fencing team this year—and maybe I'll let you go completely. If not . . . well. We'll have to let the police know about your trespassing. Not to mention . . . *the state athletic association*!" The eyes of the wrestlers in the room went wide, like this threat was just too much.

I tried to look equally traumatized by the threat, and nodded fervently. "But I can't just tell you with them in the room. They mention this online or to a friend, it'll all come back to me. I'll lose everything."

Coach considered this and then made a small flicking gesture with his hand. The wrestlers exited the room. "Stay in front of the door," Coach said. They nodded and then shut the door behind them.

"Okay—I'm going to start with the big one, okay? The thing Wellington would kill me if they knew I was telling you. It's . . . it's your ballet program," I said.

He frowned. "What?"

"Wellington's ballet program is a thousand times better, and word is that you don't appreciate yours here. Some people say you don't even think it's a real sport. So, we were supposed to recruit ballet students to come join us at Wellington. That's why we snuck into that class."

"They want my *ballet class*? I have dozens of amazing basketball players! A whole football team of all-stars! I've got gymnasts with more gold medals than I have *teeth*. And they like my ballet program?"

"Exactly. See, you forget about them. Do you know how many professional football teams there are in America?"

"Thirty-two."

"Well, there are a whole lot more professional ballet companies in the United States, and thousands more worldwide. Ballet is the big fish, and you're letting it swim away."

Coach stared at me like I was speaking total lunacy, but then he stepped forward and popped open the tape around both of my wrists. "All right. Interesting. Not enough to get you out of here, but interesting." He flipped through a few of the files Walter and I had removed from the cabinets. "These aren't ballerinas, though—not all of them anyway. These are the shining stars out of my youngest students. The kids who will practically own professional sports some day."

I shrugged at Coach. "Can't blame us for trying to get their info. We want them at Wellington."

"I'm sure you do. You know, Quincy, I think it says

something about Wellington, that you've betrayed them. That's your team! No one likes a fair-weather fan—"

I spun around, kicked off the lockers, and launched myself in the rolling chair toward my lunch bag. Coach dived for me just as I got my hands in the bag, but I grabbed the first one of Ben's inventions that I could, hoping that it was the BEN Seeing You. I mashed the button on it as I pulled my hand out.

A tent popped open out of nowhere with so much force that it threw me against the cubbies and Coach against his desk—the CaBEN. I grimaced, looked at the belt, and snatched the BEN Seeing You from its pouch. I ducked under the tent and, while Coach was busy processing the fact that his office was suddenly a campsite, pressed it up against his arm and hit the button at the end. There was a small *pop*, and before I could even worry about what the sound meant, Coach was on the floor in a heap, breathing steadily. The room was quiet.

"Whoa," I said. Ben was both impressive and terrifying at the moment. I wondered who he'd tested this thing on.

I glanced up at the door as I hurriedly peeled the rest of the athletic tape off my arms and torso, flinching as it took the hair on my arms with it. I could still hear the wrestlers outside, milling around. That wasn't an option for an exit route. I glanced up. There were ceiling tiles that inevitably led to air ducts, but I didn't fit inside the ones at SRS;

there was no reason to believe these would be any different.

Focus. Think of the mission. I dumped out the rest of my lunch bag, fumbling to put on my com unit.

"Clatterbuck, you there?" I said into the bracelet as I shoved the belt down my uniform shirt. Thankfully, the black material made it look a lot less lumpy than I expected. "Clatterbuck!" I yelled again.

"Um, yep—Ben! Be quiet! Hale's talking to me! Yep, right here," Clatterbuck said, and I heard paper crumpling.

"These files . . . apparently, they're all Nelson Academy's youngest students and—"

"The best. We heard most of it," Clatterbuck said. "Look, forget the files, Hale—you've got to get out of there, and we're going to help."

"What? No! You can't. Walter's surely signaled SRS by now. If you guys cross paths, I'm . . . well. Let's just say, I'm in trouble. I promise, I can get myself out of here."

Clatterbuck made a disapproving noise. "I can try to cancel our exit plan, I guess. But it might be too late."

"Do it, Clatterbuck!" I snapped, and instantly felt a little bad about it. "Okay, write this down—maybe it'll help us figure out what SRS wants these kids' files for. Lavender Dalton, she's a gymnast, and apparently she's the only girl in the world who can do the Tkachev salto, whatever that is. Simon Bells, he's a basketball player, but, huh . . . he hasn't really been on a great team—oh! He's one of those trick-shot guys who can make a basket from anywhere. Leslie Gordon is a ballerina, she set a pirouette record—"

Coach groaned a little.

"That'll have to be enough. I've got to get out," I said swiftly. *Exit strategy, exit strategy, come on.* Only one door. No routes through the ceiling. I looked at the ground and ran my hand over it—nope, tile over what felt like solid concrete. I spun around and looked at the gray walls nearly covered in framed certificates and awards . . .

Got it.

Well, hopefully.

Mission: Escape Nelson Sports Academy without getting beaten up by a country's worth of wrestlers
Step 1: Literal smoke screen

I ran to the coffeemaker in the corner and grabbed the container of sugar—it was heavy and felt new, perfect. The potted plant on Coach's desk—there was no sunlight in here, so he had to be giving it fertilizer, or the thing would have been dead. I hurriedly opened a few of his desk drawers—yes, fertilizer. I unwound an entire roll of paper towels by the coffeemaker and stole the tube from the inside, then closed up one end with a wad of tape.

It wasn't pretty, but it would work. I poured sugar and

fertilizer in the tube, a few shakes of each, one right after the other. When it was halfway full, I paused to put a long strand of the athletic tape inside, leaving a few inches poking out of the top. I continued filling, faster, faster . . . Coach moaned again, and his fingertips were starting to move. My paper towel tube was complete; now I just needed something to light it with . . .

I ransacked Coach's drawers, but there was nothing.

"What's going on? What are you doing?" Clatterbuck asked over the com.

"Looking for something to light this explosive with."

"What?"

"Not now, Clatterbuck! I've got to think—" *Yes, that's it!*

I heaved myself up onto the desk, stood on my toes to pop off the cover on the overhead light, and held the tube against the lightbulb. It burned the tips of my fingers before the tape finally began to smoke. I pulled it down and cupped my hands around it, coaxing it into the flame. When it was going strong, I placed it by the door and then ran around and grabbed the folders SRS wanted, tucking them into the front of my uniform. I crouched down behind Coach's desk. The tape burned down and then, when it hit the sugar and fertilizer I'd mixed together in the tube, white smoke appeared. It grew thicker, thicker, thicker, and I finally heard panic on the outside of the door.

It was really just a simple smoke bomb—nothing too dangerous. But I guess they didn't really know about smoke bombs, seeing as how they went to sports school instead of spy school.

The smoke was so heavy in the room now that I couldn't see a thing, but then, I didn't need to. I waited until I heard the wrestlers fling the door open, the spray of a fire extinguisher (which only added more smoke), and a clatter of people and limbs and shouting. I waited until I felt people all around me, and then I rose and rushed for the door, hidden by the smoke and commotion.

Step 2: Get out of here

I hurried down the hall to the side door of the ballet room. It wouldn't take long for the smoke to fade, and then . . .

"Hey! Watch it!" someone snapped as I plowed into him. I stumbled, struggling to hold on to all the stolen folders, and then I face-planted into the dirt. The speaker snorted—I knew that snort.

"Walter?" I said, lifting my head. It was him.

"What'd you do in there?" he asked, looking at the smoke billowing out the side of the building.

"Smoke bomb. Thanks for all your help with that escape," I snapped, getting to my feet. My tolerance for Walter's crappy fieldwork was at an all-time low.

"Hey, I was coming back! That's why I'm here instead of at SRS!"

"You're *here* because SRS isn't sending the agent to pick us up until three!" I said as we tromped around the side of the building.

"It's not my fault—this wasn't in the mission packet! We should have planned an emergency exit. We should have—Are you wearing jewelry?"

I fought the urge to flinch—if I did, Walter might see it and realize something was up. So I rolled my eyes. "Those wrestlers did it to make fun of me. You know—sort of like how you and your friends call me Hale the Whale?"

"That's different. We're just kidding," Walter said, scoffing. We were nearly to the lower parking lot now, and I could hear shouting back at the school. I was pretty sure that at this point they'd be calling the police rather than the state athletic association.

"Yeah, a joke. It's hilarious, Walter. A real riot," I muttered, reaching up to yank the com off.

A squeal of tires. Walter and I both spun around and tensed. It was a shiny black car, like one of the dozens SRS had in their garages. I couldn't decide if I was offended—clearly, SRS thought we might fail, and they'd built in an exit strategy. But then again, we *needed* it, especially now that I could hear sirens in the distance. The car came to a screeching halt in front of us and, without missing a beat, Walter lunged for the door and leaped inside. I followed him, dragging the door shut behind me, and the driver mashed the accelerator to the ground. We fishtailed as we cut out of the parking lot and back onto the street.

"Whoa," Walter called out to the agent driving. "Won't this car give us away? What happened to the van?"

"Seriously? You seriously think the *car* is what's going to give us away?" I muttered, and Walter scowled at me.

"I'm sure it'll be fine," a woman's voice answered.

My chest went all cold. The driver's eyes flicked back to me.

It was Oleander. This wasn't SRS's exit strategy; it was The League's. Walter Quaddlebaum was in the car with The League, and I was the one responsible for it. I tried to keep my face steady; maybe Walter wouldn't even notice. There were hundreds of agents at SRS, and even though we knew them all one way or another, it was easy to get them mixed up . . .

"Wait, who are you?" Walter asked, leaning over the center console. It had duct tape on it, patching a few holes. The car's upholstery was likewise tattered—this was the League's car.

"I'm Agent Macoby," Oleander said swiftly. "I'm usually in Tactical Support? With Agent Smith?" Oleander's voice was smooth and sure—she'd even name-checked an actual Tactical Support agent, though I suspected she'd just taken a super-generic last name and run with it.

"I know Agent Smith, but then how do I not know you?

I know everyone in Tactical Support. Hale, do you know her?"

"Sure! Yeah, Agent Macoby. You don't remember?"

Walter stopped. He looked at my face for a long time.

I was a great liar—or actor, if you'd rather call it that. But Walter and I went way back, far enough back that even though we weren't friends anymore, he still knew all my tells. I saw the shock of realization in his eyes—that there was something going on with me and this stranger driving us around in a crappy car. He sat back, but his eyes kept flitting between me and Oleander. I tried to think of all the possible ways this could end.

Option one: Oleander drives us back to SRS. She can't park the car inside, because it isn't actually an SRS car. She can't come in with us, because she's the director of SRS's enemy organization. So we would be caught. I would be exposed as a double agent. Kennedy would get sent to live in the dorms and I'd meet some terrible fate.

Option one was no good. It'd have to be option two.

"Walter?" I said, reaching into my pocket. "I'm sorry about this."

"Sorry about wha—" he began, but he didn't get to finish, because I zapped him with the BEN Seeing You.

Oleander looked at me in the rearview mirror. "All right, Hale. Where to?"

CHAPTER TWENTY

"Does SRS even *have* agents who aren't kids?" Beatrix asked thoughtfully, tilting her head to one side. We were gathered around Walter in the League's gym. He was still out cold; Oleander and I had carried him down here and heaved him onto a mat. I'd asked Clatterbuck to go pick up Kennedy (which explained his race car driver costume). I figured that having another SRS person here to explain things couldn't hurt.

"Of course!" Kennedy said. "He's just a junior agent."

"Does that mean he's even better than Hale?" Beatrix asked, eyes wide that this was even possible. I pretended hearing that didn't sting, but really, a little part of my heart sank. SRS was already the Walter Quaddlebaum show, so it was kind of sad to think of The League becoming one too.

But Kennedy laughed Beatrix's question off. "No way. No

one's better than my brother; they just think they are."
The others nodded, like they should have realized this, and
that sinking part of me lifted back up. Kennedy went on.
"You know, *I'm* going to take my junior agent exam soon.
Then I can be a double agent too."

"No," I said.

"What? Why not! You get to be a double agent!"

"She has a point," Clatterbuck said. "I mean, technically,
anyway—"

"Don't encourage her!" I said, which was something
Mom always said to Dad when he was teaching Kennedy
how to back-talk in Cantonese.

"Don't encourage who?" Walter asked sleepily.

We all stopped talking. Clatterbuck, Ben, and Beatrix
each took a giant step back. Oleander, who was hanging a
little farther away from us anyhow, clasped her hands neatly
like she was preparing for a fancy business meeting. Based
on my own attempted escape from The League, Oleander
had already asked Clatterbuck to disable the sprinkler sys-
tems. I thought that wise.

Walter's eyes were still closed. "Did we . . . Were we compromised?" he asked, like he couldn't quite figure out if this
was a dream or not.

"No," I said. "But we aren't at SRS, Walter."

"Huh?"

"We're . . . at League headquarters."

Walter's eyelids snapped open and he jumped up. Or at

least, he tried to—the gym mat that he was on was squishy, so he sank, lost his footing, and toppled over to the side. Ben and Kennedy had to leap out of the way.

"Walter, stop—stop!" I shouted as he found his footing and spun around, panicked. He looked like some sort of wild animal, ready to charge at whomever he needed to in order to escape being caught. His eyes landed on Beatrix. I could see him determining she would be the easiest to barrel through. So I dived on top of him.

"Get off me!" he roared as I tackled him back onto the mat. Kennedy, seeing that he was about to get away, dived on top of me, flinging red hair all in my eyes and knocking the wind out of me.

"What are you two *doing*?" Walter shouted, trying to twist away. He sounded terrified, and I couldn't help but remember the first time I was in The League—before I knew that the scariest thing in this building was the back of the cafeteria's fridge.

"Just listen! *Walter*. Listen," I said, making my voice calm. "It's not what you think. If you just listen, we'll get off you."

Walter stopped, though I wasn't sure if it was because he was willing to listen or because he was just out of breath. Kennedy eased off me and then I slowly eased off Walter, holding my palms out like I was steadying a vase. Walter's eyes stayed on Oleander, Clatterbuck, and the twins, darting between all of them.

"They're League agents? That lady—she was our driver. She's a League agent?" he asked quietly.

"I'm actually the director," Oleander said. I cringed and then dived back on top of Walter before he had a chance to run again.

It took another ten minutes to convince him not to run, and even then, he only agreed to stand still if everyone from The League took six steps backward. It seemed a reasonable compromise.

"You're working with The League? Hale. They took your parents," Walter said, looking horrified.

"They didn't, though. That's what I'm saying. I broke into this place to look for them, and all I found were Beatrix, Ben, and a bunch of old gym equipment."

"*You* broke into League headquarters?" Walter asked, and I shrugged. He shook his head. "No, no. You're crazy. You and Kennedy both. Maybe Fishburn will let this go; maybe you're just traumatized over your parents getting compromised. I'll tell him you did well on the last mission. I'll put in a good word with Otter, even. But . . . you double-crossed SRS. Hale, you know what they do to double-crossers."

I looked over to Ben; he nodded and handed me the printout from SRS that I'd asked him to have on hand for this. I unfolded it and gave it to Walter.

"And this is what they do to their loyal agents, Walter. They put my parents In the Weeds."

Walter's eyes widened. He rubbed the paper between his fingers and then flapped it a little, trying to tell if it was a fake. When he realized it wasn't, his eyes went wider.

"SRS wants my parents dead—*my parents*. The most loyal agents in the world. *The Team*. The League aren't the bad guys—they're barely even functioning these days. Look around. This isn't an elite spy facility. It's barely even a facility. Come on, Walter—you know me, or at least, you used to. Do you really think I'm the type to do something this crazy without being sure?"

A long pause settled over the room. Then hoarsely Walter said, "No."

I took a deep breath. "All right. Well, then. This is Dr. Oleander. That's Beatrix. She's a computer genius, basically. She wrote an entire sub-program overnight a few weeks ago. And that's her brother, Ben. Ben invented the BEN Seeing You thing that I zapped you with—"

"Have you seen any spots, by the way?" Ben asked.

"Uh, no," Walter answered.

"Oh. Well, if you see some spots, don't worry. It's all part of the process."

"Great," Walter said, sounding defeated. His eyes rose to Clatterbuck.

"And I'm Stan Clatterbuck, their uncle," Clatterbuck said, grinning broadly and extending a hand to Walter. I probably should have suggested he take his race car driver costume off before making the introduction.

Walter shook Clatterbuck's hand weakly, like the man was maybe just a figment of his imagination. I sighed. "Can I talk to Walter alone for a minute, guys?"

Everyone nodded.

"Nice to meet you, Walter!" Beatrix called out as they filed out of the gym. "Hale, could you check the time when he sees those spots? We need to log it!"

I walked over and dropped down on the mat beside Walter. He kept folding and unfolding the SRS printout.

"I know it's hard to believe."

Walter finally put the printout down. "I always wondered why I couldn't be a chef."

I blinked. This was not the response I'd expected.

Walter continued, "I mean, I'm not saying I want to be a chef. But I get nervous in the field, and then it took me ages and ages to even be able to do half the physical stuff, and I'm still no good with languages, and I just . . . I always wondered if I could be something else. So one time I asked my mom."

"What'd she say?"

"She said that I was going to be an SRS agent, and that was all there was to it. Then she said I should be more like you, actually. Even when you were terrible at something, you were always trying to get better at it. You always cared so much. You wanted to be a field agent so bad."

"Yeah, and look where all that got me," I scoffed. "My parents are In the Weeds, my sister and I are traitors, and I still can't run a mile."

"But you still quit SRS," Walter said.

I didn't know what to say.

"Anyhow," Walter went on, "ever since then I've wondered what kind of place doesn't let people quit. So I guess it's not really surprising that the answer is: a bad place."

Walter looked around, taking in the crappy gym equipment, the closet full of Ben's inventions, the outdated fitness posters on the walls. "Did you know League headquarters looked like this before you broke in?"

"No," I answered. "I was expecting SRS. But The League hasn't had a mission in years."

Walter frowned. "They must be doing *some* sort of spying on us, though. That Oleander lady knew Agent Smith was in Tactical Support."

"Smith? That was a lucky guess on a common name. Seriously, Walter—it's nothing like we thought. No heavy artillery, no war rooms, no undercover ops, no junior agents, even. The League is just . . . well . . . *this*," I said, motioning to the dilapidated gym.

Walter licked his lips as he looked around. "So. You thought The League was everything we've been told, and you came anyway. Wow, Hale. Imagine what Michael and Cameron would think if they knew—"

I cringed at the mention of the Foreheads. "You can't tell them. Walter, you can't tell anyone. It's too dangerous."

Walter lifted an eyebrow. "People should know, Hale. I

mean, this changes everything. Besides, you told Kennedy. Can't I tell my mom?"

"No—she might already know, Walter. She might be in on the whole thing. She's assistant director! There's no way to know for sure. We can't risk it."

Walter opened his mouth to argue, but then he shut it firmly. He looked crushed, but he knew I was right. He licked his lips again, and then said, "Okay, but clearly, none of the kids at SRS know. I bet some of the junior agents could help you. I mean, if some of those guys knew about you breaking in here, if they realized what all you've done—"

"I'm sure they'd still find plenty of reasons to call me Hale the Whale," I cut him off, growing frustrated. "I'm not trusting my life with a bunch of jerks who hate me, Walter."

Walter's face dropped. It was a long time before he spoke, and when he did, he was quiet. "Look, Hale. I didn't mean to stop being your friend last year, exactly. I just . . . all of a sudden, I was good at things. It was, like, all that time I spent worrying about being a disappointment . . . Suddenly it didn't matter. Do you know what that's like? And then they wanted me to be their friend, and all of a sudden people were looking up to me and liking me and wanting to hang out with me."

"I wanted to hang out with you from the start."

"I know. It's just . . . it's not that easy, I guess. When everything you've ever tried to be falls into your lap, it's hard to let things stay the way they've always been. It was nice to be . . . Well, cool. It was nice to be cool for once. And we really were just kidding most of the time, like I said earlier."

"It wasn't funny," I answered, folding my arms, and Walter turned an uneasy shade of pink.

"Yeah . . . I just . . . well, I'm sorry. I really am. I've been sorry for a long time, actually, but I just didn't know how to say it."

Here was the thing: Walter was a jerk. I mean, I knew it, and I was sure he knew it. There wasn't really anything he could say to me to undo all the times he'd called me Fail Hale alongside the Foreheads the past year. It would take a long time for me to get over that. But even though I wasn't ready to be Walter's friend again, we at least had to watch each other's back—because we were on the same team now, like it or not. I exhaled. "Come on."

"Where are we going?"

"Oleander probably had the receptionist order pizza. I don't think she knows what else kids eat."

"You get *pizza* here?" Walter asked incredulously as he rose and followed me out the door.

CHAPTER TWENTY-ONE

Kennedy snuck back into SRS through one of the service elevators. Since Walter and I had supposedly been on a mission that went very, very south, we had to come back in through the front door and pretend like we'd only just made it back from Nelson Academy. Fishburn and Otter jumped on us immediately, demanding explanations. It was an astoundingly easy story—we just told the truth, save for the very last part about how we got away. I watched Walter carefully, worried he would crack and tell them about The League, but no. He held it together, spinning a story about how we got a ride back to SRS via a friendly cabdriver and three train stowaways.

"You mean to tell me that Hale Jordan is fast enough and strong enough to jump on a moving train?" Otter asked witheringly.

"I helped him," Walter snorted. *"Obviously."*

I grimaced. We'd agreed that it would look suspect for Walter to suddenly stop mocking me, which meant back at SRS, he was still the same old Walter who everyone had come to expect in the past year.

"We got these, though," I said, pulling the stolen files from my uniform and handing them to Fishburn.

"Oh!" Fishburn said, surprised. "Is this all of them?" I nodded. "Well. This is a huge step for Operation Evergreen then, though I can't say I'm very pleased to hear you two wrecked what was supposed to be a clean mission. Nelson Sports Academy is on every news station in the country."

"Sorry, sir," Walter and I said in unison.

"Still, I'm impressed that you managed to get out, and even more impressed that you kept your identities and the information private. Well done, both of you. Now . . . we'll continue to work on Operation Evergreen, but at this point, I'd like for you both to help us out with an upcoming mission."

"Sir," Otter said stiffly. "Hale Jordan *still* hasn't passed his junior agent exam—"

"Yes, yes, I know. But he's done quite well in the field thus far. I'd like to continue this experiment. Perhaps our physical requirements need to be reevaluated," Fishburn said.

Otter looked like he very much wanted to bury himself in some sort of hole. Fishburn ignored him.

"We'll be giving out briefings on the new project over the next few days. It's exciting work, though—and your particular role involves parts *only* people your age can play, so we're very fortunate to have so many trained and qualified junior agents. I'm looking forward to it," Fishburn said.

"What's the new project called, sir? If you don't mind my asking," Walter asked.

Fishburn had already returned to reading the thick stack of papers on his desk. "The upcoming one? It's called Project Groundcover."

Walter and I walked back toward the apartments in near silence. I could tell he was still processing everything, and even though I wanted to ask—just to make sure—if he planned on telling anyone about The League, I decided I had to just trust that he wouldn't. It wasn't easy, and my stomach was swirling when we split off and I finished the trek to our apartment alone.

Inside, I heard the screech of tape being pulled off a roll. I frowned and pushed the door open.

"What are you doing?" I asked, a deadened mixture of horror and anger ripping through me. It was Ms. Elma. She was in the middle of our living room, taping shut a box that, if the label on the side was accurate, was full of JUNK FROM THE LIVING ROOM DRAWERS.

"Calm down, Hale. You knew my staying here was only temporary."

"So you're packing up our apartment?" I shouted. I rushed over and stepped between her and the box of my parents' things.

"We're just putting things in storage for now. As soon as your parents are found, we'll help them move everything back—"

I hollowed with realization. Packing up our apartment, moving on . . . Did this mean SRS had finally found and killed my parents? My voice shook violently. "Wait—has anything happened? Did we hear anything about them?"

"No!" Ms. Elma said. "There's been no news. But I need to get back to my own responsibilities, so I can't babysit you any longer. You and Kennedy will need to move into the dorms."

Kennedy suddenly emerged from her bedroom, face puffy and tear-stained.

"She says I have to put all my posters in a box," she said, spitting the words at Ms. Elma.

"Don't worry," I said. "It's just temporary, okay? They won't be there long."

This did little to console Kennedy, who had a meltdown at the idea of putting any of her posters in boxes. I helped her take down her posters and carefully roll them, and together we selected which of her many pom-poms could be packed and which had to stay with her. Ms. Elma continued to pack up the living room and kitchen, treating things so casually that I almost—and I *mean* almost— went and used the BEN Seeing You on her. When she started toward my parents' bedroom with a giant box in hand, I stopped her.

"Don't touch their things. I'll do it," I said, and to my surprise, Ms. Elma looked startled—maybe even a little afraid.

"I'll help," Kennedy said. Ms. Elma glanced in Kennedy's room and saw it was still mostly a mess of neon and doll hair, but she shrugged and went back to packing up our silverware. I shut the door to our parents' room so that we couldn't hear the sound of the clanging, and Kennedy and I stared, unsure where to start.

"Maybe just the boring stuff first," she finally said. "Like the socks."

That seemed liked a good enough place, so we put the box between us, opened our parents' sock drawer, and then began slowly dropping the socks in one at a time.

"Hale. I'm going to pass my junior agent test tomorrow."

"Of course you will. You're great," I said, trying to smile.

"And when I do, you have to let me help you at . . . The . . ." She didn't say the word "League" out loud, which I appreciated. "You have to. Otherwise there's no point to me being a junior agent at all, because I'm *not* going to help SRS. I don't want to be a bad guy."

I stopped, fiddling with the sock in my hands. "It's just that it's so dangerous, Kennedy. You're only nine."

"You're only twelve."

"You still sleep with a stuffed hedgehog."

"Don't bring Tinsel into this," she said.

"Okay, you're really, um . . . small?"

"And you don't look much like a spy yourself," Kennedy said, but she said so in a way that was totally unlike the way Otter would have said it. She tilted her chin up proudly. "But it's okay, Hale. Real heroes don't always look like heroes, remember?"

For my little sister, she was awfully smart sometimes.

The SRS dormitories were above the cafeteria and, truth be told, they weren't horrible. Everyone had their own very tiny bedroom, with a shared shower for boys and another for girls at the end of the hall.

"It'll be all right, Kennedy. You're down the hall in room twenty-three thirty-four. Want me to carry your bag?" Agent Farley asked—he was this week's dorm parent. Kennedy shook her head, and I gave Agent Farley a sort of meek smile before he turned around and walked away. Kennedy and I made our way toward her room, past dozens of open doors. Inside each, watching us knowingly, were familiar faces—people from various grades who I knew by virtue of how small a community SRS was, but also Emily, one of Kennedy's friends, and Stewart and Merilee, who were twins in my class. Emily dashed from her room to hug Kennedy tightly as we made our way down the hall.

"It's not so bad here," Emily whispered before releasing her. Kennedy didn't seem to really hear her, whereas I felt like I was hearing Emily's voice over and over in my head. Not her words, exactly, but how sad she sounded. Here was a whole floor of kids whose parents were gone, some forever, and for what? They might have been just like our parents—they might have not realized SRS was evil. Or maybe they *had* realized, and that was why they'd been eliminated.

I never thought I had anything at all in common with the dorm kids, but now they were more like Kennedy and me than anyone else in this horrible place. I swallowed, because if I didn't, I might have shouted everything I knew. Just run through the halls, yelling it, telling everyone, warning them that the organization they worked for was nothing like it seemed . . .

"Do you want help setting your room up?" I asked Kennedy as I dropped her off at her door. I tried to sound somewhat upbeat, but I failed pretty miserably.

"No," she said. She opened the door, and my gut twisted—she hadn't unpacked anything. The room looked stark, white, and entirely un-Kennedy-like. "We're not staying here long anyway."

"Shhh," I said, grateful that the agent who'd just walked by had had headphones on. "But . . . you're right. I'm just down the hall if you need me, okay? I'll leave my door unlocked." Kennedy nodded and then hugged me tightly before disappearing into her miserable-looking room.

I went down to my own room, which was at the end of the boys' half of the hall. Just as I was opening my door, I heard shuffling upstairs. I looked up and frowned. I knew there were more dorms up there, but they'd always just been used for storage. I glanced down the hall to make sure no one would catch me, and then I snuck into the connecting stairwell and up to the next level. Once there, I pressed my ear to the door. Nothing. I dared to push the door open.

"Hale Jordan!" a woman snapped. I leaped backward, nearly tumbling down the stairs in surprise.

"Mrs. Quaddlebaum!" I said. "I'm sorry—I just heard someone up here and thought I'd look—"

"You're supposed to be in your room," she said, folding her arms.

"Well, yeah, but I heard someone up here and . . . I was just curious." I didn't dare take my eyes off Mrs. Quaddlebaum, but with my peripheral vision I could sort of see the hall behind her. The lights were all on, and the room had the lemony scent of a space freshly cleaned. Why were they cleaning this level? There were plenty of rooms downstairs.

"Just clearing out some rooms," she said sternly. "Now go on. I'll let you slide on being out past curfew, since I'm assuming you just didn't know the dorm rules. It is your first day in the dorm, right?"

I nodded.

Mrs. Quaddlebaum pointed, and I began to retreat down the steps. As I left, she called after me. "We're doing everything we can to find your parents, Hale, so hopefully you won't be in those dorms for long," she said in a rare show of something resembling sympathy.

I turned and gave her a fake smile even the Body Language Analysis teacher wouldn't have been able to see through. "I'm sure I won't be."

CHAPTER TWENTY-TWO

The following day I lost the race at the end of class, as per usual.

Walter jeered me along with the others, as per usual.

And I spent a lot of time thinking about Groundcover, as per usual.

Otter, who was still bitter about the whole hospital thing, sent me out to dry-clean all his heavy winter coats (I was almost positive they weren't even his. I think he just collected them from the Wardrobe Department because he knew they'd practically break my arm off when I carried them to the dry cleaner). It was obnoxious, but at least it meant I had a legitimate excuse to leave SRS instead of sneaking out again. Clatterbuck, dressed as a farmer, picked me up in a truck filled to the brim with watermelons.

"Isn't Oleander going to be mad that you keep spending

The League's little bit of money on things like costumes and watermelons?"

Clatterbuck shrugged. "She doesn't care what I spend the money on, Hale, so long as it means keeping you safe. You're our most important asset."

I blushed, hating myself for it, and said, "To be totally fair, I'm your only asset."

"No! We still have a field agent out in Japan. I mean, we haven't heard from him in seventeen years, and we're pretty sure he sold off the agency car to pay some gambling debts, but . . . he's there."

At League headquarters, Oleander and I wondered about Groundcover together for a while, and then Ben showed me a few new devices he'd made for my utility belt—which he'd also finished the auto-close clips for, so it now fit around my waist nicely. There was the RoBEN, a little windup bird that delivered a high-decibel shriek that could shatter even bulletproof glass, and the HellBENder, which he didn't much explain beyond telling me that it was only to be used as a last resort. He also had more jewelry com units, one each for Kennedy and Walter.

"So, these really are the only ones The League has that will work given how far underground SRS is. I did upgrade them a little though."

"It's going to be hard to sell Walter on wearing earrings," I said. "But thanks, Ben."

"No problem," he said, looking pleased with himself.

"Beatrix helped, though. She had to recode part of the old software."

"Where is Beatrix anyhow?" Oleander asked.

"I don't know. She took Uncle Stan's wallet to go get sodas earlier, but that was ages ago," Ben answered. Clatterbuck patted his pants pocket and looked alarmed to see his wallet was missing. "She didn't pickpocket you—you left it on the counter when you changed into your farmer overalls."

"Oh! I figured farmers don't carry wallets when they're working in the field," Clatterbuck told me.

Ben shouted Beatrix's name, and we continued to pore over the blueprints. When she didn't come, he went upstairs to the cafeteria and then down to the gym to look for her. When she wasn't in either, all four of us went searching.

"Maybe she's in the . . ." Clatterbuck finally said, giving Ben a mysterious look.

"Should we show them?" Ben answered. "If she's not there, she'll be mad we showed them without her."

"I'll be mad if you *don't* show me whatever you're talking about," Oleander said, folding her arms, a serious look on her face.

Ben and Clatterbuck didn't seem particularly happy about it, but they led Oleander and me upstairs to the door of the mission control room Oleander had shown me the day I broke in. I remembered it well enough—full of old computers and abandoned chairs and enough dust bunnies to make a pterodactyl nest. Clatterbuck and Ben grinned at each other and then swept the door open.

"Whoa," Oleander and I said in unison.

The chairs were gone, as were the dust bunnies. The old computers appeared to have been fixed up and fused together, much like Beatrix's Right Hand, and were now displaying a projected map on the back wall. There were several stations constructed out of desks, and the mission director's platform appeared to have been repainted.

"We fixed it!" Ben said jubilantly. "It was supposed to be a surprise for after we found your parents, Hale. We thought maybe they could come here and we could start running actual missions again."

"This is amazing," Oleander said.

She was right. I mean, sure, it still looked a little shabby compared to SRS's control room, but . . . this place was real. It wasn't built on lies and tricks and physical exams. There was still a sort of dark place in my heart, the reminder that when all was said and done, SRS wouldn't be my home anymore. But seeing a real mission control room here at The League . . .

"It's perfect," I said.

"Well, not exactly. Because Beatrix hasn't programmed those computers yet. And also, she's not here," Ben said, shaking his head. "I don't get it."

Clatterbuck and Oleander glanced at each other warily,

each trying to gauge how serious the other thought this whole thing was. I wasn't worried—Beatrix was tiny, so it seemed pretty plausible she was tucked away somewhere, totally absorbed in some sort of computer-genius-type work. I was about to suggest we check the upper empty floors, when Clatterbuck suddenly grabbed for his ear. Someone was talking to him over his com unit.

"Whoa. Slow down—actually, hang on. Ben, can you transfer this to the overhead speaker yet?"

"Sure thing," Ben said. He ran to one of the stations and flipped a few switches up. There was a sharp buzzing noise, but then . . .

"Hale? Are you there? Can anyone hear me?" Walter's voice boomed through the overhead speaker. Ben winced and turned it down a little.

"Yeah! What's going on?" I called out.

"Well, I was on my way to do an extra jujitsu session, and I heard my mom's voice from down the hall. So I was just curious, and I stick my head around the corner to look, and she's leading this line of people—*kids* our age. New kids, not SRS kids."

"New kids? Like, strangers? Why are strangers—"

"One of them is Beatrix, Hale! Beatrix is *here*."

"What do you mean she's *there*?" I asked.

"I mean she's here! She's with them!"

Ben and Clatterbuck spun around to look at me. My

mouth dropped open, but my mind immediately began to whir. Beatrix. Beatrix was at SRS, and we had to get her out. We had to plan.

I said, "Okay. They somehow must have caught her helping me. Maybe her program at the hospital—"

Walter cut me off, "Hale, this can't be you. If they knew she was a part of the whole doublecross, then things would be a lot . . . um . . . worse. Plus, why bring in a dozen new kids if Beatrix is the problem? I think this is Operation Evergreen—I recognize one of the kids whose file we stole from the sports academy. The gymnast, I think. And one of the other kids I remember seeing back on my first mission at that chess tournament—"

"They're recruiting," Oleander said suddenly.

The three of us spun to face her. She puffed her lips for a moment, like she couldn't believe this hadn't occurred to her before. "SRS has always been immensely private. They've ensured loyalty by having families working there. But eventually everyone needs new blood. So they collected hospital records. Files from sports academies."

"Chess championship information," I said, remembering Walter's first mission.

"Exactly. Everything you've done for Operation Evergreen has involved tracking exceptional kids."

"Beatrix said she saw her files getting transferred to SRS . . . The doctors must have written down that she was a computer genius, like they wrote down stuff about Clifton Harris . . ." I felt guilty for not seeing this before, but how could I have? SRS *never* brought in new people.

"Are you two saying they're going to turn my sister into an SRS agent?" Ben asked.

Walter crackled over the speaker again. "Your sister and about fifteen others, I think. Let me go—I'm going to try to follow them and find out more. I'll keep an eye on her, Ben. Don't worry." Walter's voice vanished, replaced by the steady sound of static.

I took a deep breath. "He's right, Ben. Don't worry. Beatrix isn't going to become an agent, because we're going to get her out," I said.

"We can't," Oleander said.

Ben and Clatterbuck's mouths dropped.

"Not yet," Oleander continued, holding out her palms like it might calm Ben and his uncle down. "She's fine. They're not hurting her. Hale, you sneak out of SRS all the time—but they know you, and they trust you. No one blinks an eye if they don't see you for a few hours, because they just assume you're studying or at home or the library. But if a new recruit vanishes? They're going to notice quickly that she's gone. Then they're going to want to know how she escaped. Then they're going to check video feeds. They're going to see Beatrix leaving, but they're also going to see you and Walter and Kennedy going and coming way too often to ignore. The whole doublecross will be blown. We won't get the chance to work out Groundcover, and we definitely won't get any closer to finding your parents, Hale."

"So you're saying we just leave her there?" I couldn't believe what I was hearing and, from the looks on Clatterbuck's and Ben's faces, neither could they.

"I'm saying, Hale, that this might be our only chance. The odds of you breaking Beatrix out of SRS without revealing yourself, Walter, or Kennedy are very slim. Once you're gone, you're gone, and we'll never get a chance to look at that place from the inside again. If she's not in any real, present danger, I think we should wait it out a bit, just until we've sorted out Groundcover. The three of you can look after her, and if anything goes wrong, you have my word that we'll go in and get her." She turned now to Clatterbuck and Ben. "SRS are better than we are. There're more of them, they're better funded, they're better trained, and they're better equipped. Hale's doublecross is the only card we have to play. If we let it go too soon, we'll have nothing."

"But *they'll* have my niece," Clatterbuck said.

"Say the word, Stan, and we'll get her," Oleander answered, her voice heavy.

"We should ask her!" Ben said before his uncle could respond. We turned to him. He took a deep breath, and continued. "Let's just ask Beatrix what she wants to do."

CHAPTER TWENTY-THREE

By the time I got back to SRS, everyone was talking about the new kids. Who they were, where they'd come from, why Fishburn thought we needed new people. The junior agents were especially prickly about the entire thing.

"I'm just saying, we've been doing this *since we were born*. How are some random kids going to do better than *us*?" I heard a girl whispering loud enough for everyone to hear.

"Maybe that's the thing, though. Maybe some random kids actually are better than us," another said, worried.

"No way," another said.

"I heard they're from the CIA."

"Someone told me the FBI trained them."

"You know MI6? They're from a secret division called MI9."

"That's impossible. I heard them talking. They're not British."

"You don't think a spy trained by MI9 could fake an American accent?"

Even the adults were swapping rumors. In every version, SRS had recruited the kids or rescued them from terrible homes or orphanages or, according to one of the Foreheads, off a sinking ship. I didn't hear a shred of the truth—or anything about Operation Evergreen.

Mrs. Quaddlebaum was guarding the new recruits carefully; people could talk to them, but only for a few seconds at a time, and then we were hurried off. I finally saw Beatrix, whose face lit up a little too much when she saw me. I lifted my eyebrows, and she quickly dropped her grin.

"Hi—you're new here?" I asked warmly. She and the others were in line near the nurse's office, apparently getting blood drawn and their tonsils checked. Beatrix was toward the back of the line, leaning against the wall. As promised, she didn't look particularly scared and certainly wasn't hurt.

"Yep, today. Are *you* one of the spies? We've been recruited to become spies too, just like on TV. We're gonna be heroes!" she said all this quickly, giving me as much information as she dared with Mrs. Quaddlebaum so close by.

I gave her an appreciative nod before saying, "Sort of. I'm a spy in training. Are you guys staying in the dorms? In the brand-new rooms?"

"I think so—they look new, anyway. The whole hall is just us," she said, and then gestured to the other recruits.

"Oh yeah, which room did you get?"

"I think it's . . . thirty-three thirty-seven?"

I sucked air through my teeth. "Oh, tough break. That one's haunted. Should've gone with thirty-three thirty-*four*."

"Hale Jordan," Mrs. Quaddlebaum said, walking over. I *knew* she'd been listening in. "There is not a single place in this building that's haunted. Stop picking on the poor girl. Don't worry, Bernice—"

"Beatrix," Beatrix said.

Mrs. Quaddlebaum waved her hands like Beatrix's name was a matter of opinion. "Right. Don't listen to him. Hale, I expected better from you, picking on a classmate!"

I badly wanted to ask her where her lectures were when Walter was picking on me, but I figured this really wasn't the time. "She's joining our classes then?"

"Well, *she's* not. She's going to join the HITS, I believe. Right? Oh, there are too many of you. I can't remember who is doing what. Come on, everyone! We're going to go look at one of the Explosives classrooms now, then we'll be done with the tour and get some dinner. Let's move along!" She sounded cheery, which was weird and made it feel like she was Mrs. Quaddlebaum in shallow cover as Mrs. Cheery Quaddlebaum.

She put an arm around Beatrix and led her away quickly, back to the others. Beatrix glanced over her shoulder, and

I mouthed *room three-three-three-four*. I couldn't tell if she understood my plan, but I didn't have the chance to work it out, since they disappeared around the corner.

That night Walter and I sat in Kennedy's dorm room—room 2334—which was still sparse and sad-looking. I could tell the whole place made Walter feel awkward about how he was going to get to go home to his own bedroom, with his mom, in his own apartment, mainly because that was how I would've felt, visiting the dorm kids.

"What if Beatrix didn't understand?" Kennedy sighed, fiddling with one of the fake diamonds on her League com unit. I'd given Walter his too, but he'd quickly pocketed it like it was just too gross to look at. Ben had hurriedly set up a final one for me to give to Beatrix as well.

"I don't know," I answered Kennedy. "We'll have to figure out another way to talk with her alone—"

A knocking noise stopped us—a noise coming from overhead. I grinned and crossed my fingers that I wasn't just misinterpreting the sound of someone arranging furniture. Walter hoisted Kennedy up onto his shoulders (where she wanted to stop and practice some sort of cheerleading move). She popped out one of the ceiling tiles and passed it down to me.

Walter handed her the laser saw I'd stolen earlier from the tactical supply closet, and we all cringed as it buzzed to life. Kennedy sliced through the floor of the room above. She pushed it up and, to our relief, we saw Beatrix above, helping lift the floor out. Room 3334—right above Kennedy's room, 2334.

"Hi, guys!" she whispered, waving down at us. She set the piece of her floor aside, and Kennedy hopped down. It took a little more convincing for Beatrix to jump down into Walter's arms, but she eventually did it, looking very pleased with herself as he caught her squarely. I hugged her tightly as soon as she stepped down.

"I'm okay," she assured me when I let her go. "Hale! I'm fine, I promise. Really good idea about the ghost, by the way. I told Mrs. Quaddlebaum I was scared, then cried until she let me switch with the girl who had this room."

"Oh yeah, she hates crying," Walter said sagely. Beatrix plopped down on Kennedy's bed and, though she didn't say it aloud, I could tell even she thought this room was entirely un-Kennedy.

"All right. So, you want to know how I ended up here?" she said, and we nodded. "It's actually pretty basic. Remember how I saw them looking through my and Ben's hospital records? Well, I saw that they were sorting them and pulling out the records that had notes in them—you know: 'this kid plays hockey!' and 'this kid prefers to go by "Junior"' and 'this kid won a science fair!' So I went ahead and put stuff in my file—you know, how I won a programming contest once, and how I figured out a better algorithm for filtering out Internet spam, things like that, just to see what would happen."

"You won a programming contest?" Walter asked.

"Yes, but I got disqualified because it was supposed to only be for Germans. Anyway, these guys in suits stopped me on my way to the grocery store to get sodas, and then one of them stuck me with some sort of knockout gas, and then . . . I woke up here with all the other kids. One of them is the best chess player *in the world*. Seriously. Apparently, they flew him in from Belgium."

"How are they not freaking out? How are *you* not freaking out?

"Well, they are, actually. A lot of them cried, and some of them are in shock. But they basically told us that we were geniuses, and the country needs for us to become superspies, which a lot of the others are excited about. I was sort of scared at first, but I figured that you guys were here, for one, but also that this is *great*. SRS has a closed system—I could never have hacked into their networks from the outside. But now I'm on the inside!"

"Yeah, but you're *stuck* on the inside, Beatrix!" I said, exasperated.

"How can I be stuck? You sneak out all the time," Beatrix reminded me.

I sighed and told her exactly what Oleander had told the

rest of us—how me being gone wasn't news, but a new recruit slipping out?

Beatrix's face fell.

"I guess I didn't think of that," she said, folding her arms over her chest. Her pride seemed to be deflating, and Walter looked very worried she might cry. "What are we going to do?" Beatrix asked as Kennedy patted her back.

"We'll get you out of here, Beatrix. But Oleander thinks we should wait. Once they realize I'm double-crossing them, I can never come back. This is our last chance to learn about Groundcover."

"So . . . I ruined everything?" Beatrix asked, and her voice cracked a tiny bit. "I thought I was helping. I'm sorry. I'm so sorry. I didn't mean—"

"No, no. You're right—now that you're here, you can break into their system. You can help us figure out Groundcover, and then we're all safe to leave. But . . . it'll mean you have to stay here a few days while I figure out a plan. It's your choice. Do you want to escape now, or do you want to wait?"

Beatrix shifted a little. "I can wait," she said, and then looked at Kennedy. "Can we leave the floor open, though, in case I get homesick?"

"Of course," Kennedy said, and we all nodded in relief. We had more time, even if it was only a little.

"What about my mom? What happens to her when we break Beatrix out?" Walter interrupted my thoughts.

Kennedy snorted, like Walter was being ridiculous. "She'll be fine. It's not like we're breaking Beatrix out with guns and grenades or anything."

"I know *that*," Walter said. "I meant—I can't exactly tell her about all this, because for all we know, she's in on it. But what if she really doesn't know anything, even though she's assistant director? I can't just *leave* her here . . ."

"You'll have to," I said firmly, but I hoped not unkindly. There was no other way, though. We were also leaving the dorm kids and Kennedy's friends and plenty of other people who I strongly suspected had no idea about what SRS was. It wasn't something I wanted, or something I felt good about, but it was the only way I could safely get out everyone I cared about.

Walter faltered for a second, opening his mouth like he was going to argue, but then he shut it in a firm line.

His voice shook a little as he said, "I just wish there was a way to show everyone at SRS the stuff on Groundcover and Evergreen. Show them how your parents are In the Weeds. That way there're no more secrets. People can choose their sides, and we don't have to worry about innocent people being stuck here."

I nodded. "Maybe . . . Beatrix, do you think you could leave yourself some sort of back door into the system? And then once we've read the Groundcover files, we can send them to every computer here or something—"

Beatrix was shaking her head. "They'll find it and shut it down before we can even read the files."

"Right," I said, sighing. "We'll find a way to tell them eventually, Walter. If we have to drop in on missions and hand them little scraps of paper that say, 'SRS is evil!' then we will. Okay?"

"Thanks," Walter said, and kind of half smiled. He still looked worried, but I guess that was to be expected. I knew how he felt. Knowing the truth was a lot harder than believing the lie.

Walter and I returned to our rooms. I could hear Beatrix talking to Ben over her com unit—I guess we didn't have different channels—so I waited until she was done to get one and ask for Clatterbuck and Oleander. I updated them on everything and told them I was going to work on a plan.

Oleander didn't sound very excited—I guess because our team was five kids and an ex-agent who, last I saw him, was dressed as a race car driver. "It just can't go wrong, Hale. If it's too risky, we should wait. You know how missions work. The more moving parts, the more things to break."

I agreed with her 100 percent, and told her so. An hour later I pulled the sheets on my bed tightly and began drawing my finger across them, formulating plans without ever actually putting a pen to paper, since the last thing I needed was hard evidence. There was no way to make this simple. We needed stuff from the Disguise Department. We needed access to the SRS cameras. We needed a cheer-leading squad. One wrong move and we'd all likely be In the Weeds.

Easy enough.

We just couldn't make a single wrong move.

CHAPTER TWENTY-FOUR

Kennedy had to do the impossible for the plan to even get off the ground: finally convince Fishburn that SRS badly needed a cheerleading squad.

I had to admit that this was the strangest start to a mission I'd ever heard of, much less ever planned. It was also perhaps the most difficult, the most time sensitive, and the most specific—because let's face it: this was something only Kennedy could do. No matter what sorts of missions I'd gone on recently, Fishburn would still be incredibly suspicious if *I* came to him with a burning desire for pom-poms.

In the meantime, there was nothing for me to do but wait. SRS kept the recruits pretty far away from the rest of us. According to Beatrix, they were suffering through a crash course in everything SRS, which was taught by Mrs. Quaddlebaum and a few other senior agents. Since she was slated to become a HITS anyway, they'd allowed Beatrix to skip all the physical stuff and go straight to the deck with the other HITS guys. It was perfect, since it meant she was already learning her way around the SRS system.

Beatrix tucked her feet under the edge of my blankets—the stupid dorms were always cold. She said, "It's genius. They have it set up so if anything triggers the system, everything shuts off. Literally, just powers down."

"What're you going to do then?" Ben said over the com unit. It was Thursday afternoon, which made me nervous since it meant so many people might overhear us, but I figured it was smart to mix up the times of our secret meetings. Still no word from Walter, and Kennedy was just finishing class, so it was just Beatrix and me, with Clatterbuck and Ben over the com unit.

"Well, I can still get *in*, but I can't change any permissions or send out any files or change anything, basically. Anything like that happens, it'll trigger a shutdown."

"Does that mean you can't crack the Groundcover file?" I asked. There was no point in Beatrix taking risks if she couldn't discover anything more than what I already knew.

"Well, it means that I *can* locate the file, but I can't pull it up on the computer I use in the control deck because none of the computers in there have that level access. It's labeled as a Gold Level file—what computers or people would have that, Hale?"

I sighed. "That's Fishburn. I hoped you'd be able to crack

it from up there, but . . . we'd have to get on his actual computer to look at it. His office is locked up and has an alarm system that I can't get past without getting caught. I wouldn't have enough time to read a single page before agents were on top of me."

"What if I printed the pages?" Beatrix asked carefully. "He has a printer in his office that I could access."

I frowned. "That'd be better—but I'd still have to break into the office and set off the alarm. We couldn't make a clean getaway . . . but . . . maybe. Let me think on it."

Beatrix nodded. "Sounds good. You know, I feel sort of bad. The HITS guys are nice. Everyone here is nice, really, except Mrs. Quaddlebaum, and even she's okay. I can see why you never realized this place was full of bad guys, Hale."

"The villains never look like villains," I said quietly, thinking about when Dad said it to me. He was right. Really, really right.

Kennedy suddenly flung open my dorm room door. She was grinning, and it was pretty heartwarming to see her cartwheel over to us, just like she would have done back when Mom and Dad were here.

"I think Fishburn's convinced!" she said, landing squarely on the bed beside Beatrix.

"How'd you do it?" I asked.

"I told him I was really sad that the new kids were all separated from us, and that we should do something to bring everyone together. And *he* said that new recruits were just having a hard time adjusting, and I was like, 'No, we should do something to show them we're fun and exciting and not really that different from them!' and he said, 'You mean like eating dinner together?' and I was like, 'No, like an *activity*,' and then he went off on this long thing about making friendship bracelets and finally I told him that cheerleading teams were basically famous for being super-close to one another. And I reminded him that most of the new recruits probably knew exactly what cheerleading was, so what if we all got together and did a performance for the rest of SRS? So in the end, he said I had to ask the new recruits first, and that I had to get at least as many kids from SRS on board to make it worth all the effort."

"And the uniforms? Did he approve uniforms?" I asked. That was the most important part.

Kennedy nodded. "He said Ms. Elma could do uniforms, but he asked me not to make them complicated, because she was already busy."

I exhaled. "Okay. Okay, this is good. Beatrix, can you convince all the new recruits to sign up? *Without* telling them what we're doing?" I hated not to let them in on our plan, but there was no way we could trust a dozen regular kids with a secret this big.

"I think so—but I'll have to tell them what we're really up to, Hale."

"No, we can't—"

Beatrix continued, her voice patient. "We've pretty much

been kidnapped. Even the ones who were excited about becoming spies are starting to get pretty freaked out. Would you want to be a cheerleader if you were being held captive by SRS?" She waited to continue until after I'd sighed and shaken my head. "I know they're not spies, but neither am I, and you trust me."

"If they say anything, we'll all be In the Weeds," I said.

"I know—and I'll make sure they know. They only have to keep it a secret for a few days, anyhow."

"*And* now we'll know that when we say *run*, they'll really run," Kennedy offered, and I nodded.

"All right, all right—tell them, but tell them as little as possible, okay? And, Kennedy, you think you can get a dozen kids from SRS? Remember that you can't count me," I told her.

She nodded. "I think so. I mean, if I can convince Dr. Fishburn, surely, I can convince other people, right?"

This proved harder than she'd thought. While plenty of kids thought cheerleading was interesting enough, far fewer were interested in participating—especially since it wasn't entirely clear what they'd be cheering *for*. Still, she managed to get six girls and two boys from her own class, and then Walter helped her convince a few junior agents. Once Beatrix got the recruits on board—which she said was indeed easy, once they knew being a cheerleader would mean going home—Ms. Elma began working on the cheerleading uniforms. She liked to loudly complain about them whenever Kennedy, I, or Fishburn were within earshot. I couldn't exactly blame her; going from sewing bullet-proof panels into ball gowns to making cheerleading skirts was probably a little insulting.

The cheerleading squad was just one part of all the preplanning that had to be done. We also needed a new device from Ben, one that he'd stayed up all night—literally—to invent. Clatterbuck, dressed as a sandwich cart guy, delivered it to me the following morning. He handed it off while pretending to sell me a grilled cheese on whole wheat (which was delicious). I couldn't use Ben's creation right away, of course—the HITS guys would notice. I'd have to plug it in at the last possible moment. Ben called it the BENoculars, which I thought was a pretty clever name.

Finally, on the night before my plan truly went into action, Kennedy and I were in the Disguise Department. I was pretending to tutor her on artificial beard application. Secretly, we were stuffing our backpacks full of supplies we'd need the following day.

"Think we need a neck prosthetic?" Kennedy whispered while dabbing spirit gum along her jawline. She had half a long bristly beard on, and it looked pretty excellent except that it was on a nine-year-old girl.

"I think so," I answered. "Take two just in case. Is the cheerleading routine done?"

"We've practiced every day this week. We're really good! I wish we could go compete somewhere. I think we'd do okay. I mean, we probably wouldn't place, but still. Walter does this really cool stunt with one of the girl chess players."

"I'm sorry I'll miss it," I told her.

"It's okay. You're sort of saving our parents and all," Kennedy answered. "Besides, I think we're going to get it on video."

The next morning I got up early. I wasn't going to class today, but I needed to make it look like I was. I packed my bag carefully, putting everything we'd stolen from the Disguise Department into the main section. At eight o'clock, I put on the League com unit to check in with everyone like we'd planned.

"It's Hale. Everyone here?"

Ben, Beatrix, and Kennedy said hello, then Clatterbuck, who added, "And Dr. Oleander is here with me. Her com got broken last night, so—"

"*You* broke my com last night," I heard Oleander say in a very firm voice.

"I thought they were waterproof!" Clatterbuck protested.

"*Anyway*," Ben said, then cleared his throat. "League base to field agents—let's get started."

CHAPTER TWENTY-FIVE

Mission: Figure out Project Groundcover/Save Beatrix/
Save the new recruits/Escape SRS
Step 1: Install the BENoculars

The BENoculars were maybe Ben's most clever invention yet. They looked like an air freshener, the kind you plug into the wall. They were actually some sort of wireless signal device. When combined with a tiny unnoticeable program Beatrix had written and installed on the SRS computers, they would transmit a signal that would give Ben access to SRS's security cameras. Of all the million and a half parts this plan involved, the BENoculars were the piece I had the most confidence in. After all, Ben's devices had never failed me before. I plugged them into an outlet in my dorm room.

"All right," Ben said through my com unit. "I see that

they're plugged in. The cameras are trying to load. They're loading. I think they're loading. Hang on—my computer froze."

I groaned and wondered if maybe I could steal a new SRS laptop to replace one of the ancient ones The League was still using.

"Got them!" Ben said triumphantly. "Wait, no. They went out again. I think you need to plug them in somewhere else. The signal just isn't able to make it through all the walls where you are. Go someplace big and open."

"The cafeteria?" Kennedy said over the com, her voice a little lost in the chatter from all the cheerleaders. The cheerleading squad's debut performance would take place during lunch today, which meant they'd get out of class early to get ready.

Beatrix, however, was on the command deck with the HITS guys, just as she was most days, so she had to whisper, "The cafeteria is too low, probably."

"Hang on," I said. I rooted through my trash can and removed the aluminum foil wrapper that Clatterbuck gave me with my sandwich at his pretend food truck. I tore along the edges until it was a circle, and then curved it into a cone shape. With a little tape, I stuck it on top of the BENoculars, where the scent would come out if it were actually an air freshener.

"Try now," I instructed Ben.

"Hey! That did it. What'd you do?"

"Boosted the antennae. Do you have eyes on every-thing?"

"Pulling them up now . . . yes. I've got every camera at SRS, as far as I can tell. Including one in an office—oh, gross, that guy is picking his nose! Oh, now he's— Oh, that is so gross—"

"Focus, Ben," I reminded him. I double-checked that the utility belt was hidden by my shirt, and then I left my dorm room. I tucked the com bracelet under my sleeve, hiding the earring by pretending I was scratching my neck whenever someone passed me in the hallway. I glanced up at the hall-way camera as I walked past it.

"I see you, Hale," Ben said. "All right—go ahead and head toward the closet to wait. You've got plenty of time. Beatrix, have the HITS guys noticed the signal from the BENoculars?"

"Nope, they don't even know to look for it. Don't forget, Hale, that SRS can still see you on the cameras too. Go ahead and head toward the bathroom."

"On my way," I said, and went down to the administra-tive wing. There I swung into one of the bathrooms and waited by the sinks.

Step 2: Wait

This was the hard part—there was nothing more for me to do. I had to sit back and let everyone else play their parts for the next few minutes. I took a deep breath and leaned against the row of sinks.

"How are the new recruits holding up, Kennedy?" Ben asked.

"They're good. Nervous, but good. I think everyone else just thinks they're nervous about the performance. Walter is calming some of them down," she said. "Is it time for me to go get Beatrix?"

Ben said, "Yep, go ahead." Then he quickly doubled back, his voice sinking. "*Whoa*, everyone. Major problem— Fishburn hasn't left his office yet."

I put a hand to my forehead. Everything would fall apart if Fishburn didn't go to the cheerleading performance.

Step 3: Break into Fishburn's office (and don't get killed doing it)

"Okay, okay, let me think," I muttered at the empty bathroom. No one was free, exactly, to go off script and come get Fishburn. Except maybe . . . "Walter," I said. "Walter will have to come get him. Kennedy, can you tell him?"

"Hey, Walter! Dr. Fishburn isn't here yet. Can you go get him?" Kennedy immediately shouted above the fray. On the coms, everyone was silent; I wished that, like Ben, I could see the expression on Walter's face. Of all the people to go off script . . .

"Sure," Walter's voice rang across Kennedy's com.

"He's going—Hale, he's running," Ben said, sounding satisfied.

"Right," Kennedy said. With both Kennedy and Walter gone from the cafeteria, the noise on the coms faded into uneasy silence. I could hear the muffled sound of Walter's feet slapping against the floor, which grew louder as he neared me. I stepped up so I could see the hallway, and we made brief eye contact as he flew past the bathroom door. *You can do it, Walter. Don't get nervous . . .* He didn't even have to *lie* to Fishburn, really, since *You're late for the cheer-leading performance!* was the truth. But based on what I saw back at Nelson Sports Academy, he still could choke.

Ben narrated. "He's at the office, Hale. Okay, he's going in . . . talking to Fishburn—yes! Fishburn's up, they're leaving, now Fishburn's locking his door. Wow, Walter looks relieved—"

"He and I both," I said, though I couldn't deny I felt kind of proud of Walter. I waited until I heard Walter and Fishburn dash past the door to let out the deep breath I'd been holding.

Ben reappeared on the com. "All right, Fishburn is nearly to the cafeteria. Hale, hold your position. Kennedy, time to clear out the HITS room—"

"You're supposed to be in *uniform,* Beatrix! And you guys are all supposed to be in the cafeteria for the performance!" Kennedy shrieked into her com unit. Well, not exactly over her com unit—she was saying this to Beatrix and the HITS guys. My com unit was suddenly filled first with the sound of grumbling, and then with the sound of computers chiming as they were shut down and locked up.

"Oh, come on! I don't want to go!" Beatrix answered.

"You have to. You promised!" Kennedy argued with her for the benefit of the HITS audience. "Go change, fast. We're starting in one minute."

"Fine, fine," Beatrix said. The sound of the cafeteria crowd grew louder in my com unit. A minute passed, then another—we were now officially behind schedule. I forced myself to breathe slower, waiting for Ben's cue . . .

"Hale, you're clear to go to the office," Ben said.

I walked from the bathroom down the hall, then stopped in front of Fishburn's now-darkened and locked office. This was it.

"All right, ready, everyone?" Kennedy called out to the other cheerleaders. The crowd hushed.

"Stand by, Hale," Ben said. A click, and suddenly an explosive remixed pop song raged over my headset. I couldn't hear Ben anymore, couldn't hear anything but the thud of the bass and pounding melody. I had to trust my gut—it was time.

I withdrew the RoBEN from my utility belt and wound the little bird up. I set it on the office window ledge and then backed up, pinning my palms to my ears. The RoBEN screeched, a sound so impossibly high that it made my sinuses hurt. Just like Ben promised, the window shattered into a thousand tiny pieces that fell to the floor like bits of rock candy.

"You're a genius, Ben," I said into my com, though I didn't know if he'd heard me, since at that exact moment the alarms went off. Lights flared, sirens wailed, and I knew every single room at SRS had identical alarms going off—letting the entire building know of a Gold Level security breach.

I didn't care.

I mean, I did, but what I *really* cared about? The thick stack of papers just ahead, resting patiently on Fishburn's printer.

Groundcover.

CHAPTER TWENTY-SIX

"All right, Hale, it looks like the HITS guys are running back to their desks . . . Yep. They see that it's you on cameras four and five. For what it's worth, they look more concerned than angry," Ben muttered in my ear. I could barely hear him over the noise on everyone else's coms. I reached through the broken window, unlocked Fishburn's door, and ran inside. I snatched the stack of still-warm papers from the printer. I badly, badly wanted to look at them, but it wasn't exactly a good time to sit down and do some reading.

"Got the file," I answered. I tucked the papers under my arm and hurried back into the hall, away from the cafeteria.

"Perfect. Uncle Stan, you're in position, right?" Ben asked.

"Dr. Oleander and I are pulling into Castlebury now, Ben, and awaiting your order!" Clatterbuck said brightly.

"Good. All right, Hale, it looks like Fishburn is about to make an announce—"

Ben was cut off by the sound of Fishburn's voice. "Attention, SRS: Hale Jordan has violated a Gold Level security entrance. Please locate and detain Hale Jordan at once. All senior and junior agents on deck. *Hale Jordan.*" He said my name the last time like he couldn't believe it. And from the murmuring I heard over Kennedy's com, no one else could believe it either.

Step 4: Hide the new recruits in plain sight

"All right, how are we looking, Kennedy?" Ben asked her.

"Hale!" Kennedy screeched, and for a second my heart stopped—but then she went on, and I realized she was yelling for effect. People had to be staring at her right now, what with her brother being the subject of a manhunt and all. "How could he? Ugh—come on, Walter. Help me find him before he does something stupider." Her voice was gravelly and rageful, almost unrecognizably so. I heard Walter shout in agreement.

"Good job, Kennedy," Ben said. "Now you and Walter have to get out of there. That Quaddlebaum woman is heading your way to collect all the new recruits," Ben said urgently.

"Come on, everyone—let's go look upstairs. I just want to find him before everyone else—maybe there's a reason. There'd *better* be a reason," Kennedy fumed loudly. "Hurry— we've got to *run*." The last word was full of weight for the new recruits.

"Perfect," Ben said. "Hale, the SRS cheerleading squad has split up into four separate search parties."

"Can you tell which one has Kennedy and Walter and the recruits?" I asked.

"Not really. They all look the same in their uniforms. The recruits should be out of the building and to you, Uncle Stan, in thirty seconds," Ben said, sounding pleased. "Fishburn is on his way back to you, Hale. Let's get you out. Take a right and go back toward the cafeteria, and you should be able to avoid the closest pack of agents," Ben said over the com. I nodded and jumped back into the hall.

Step 5: Get the recruits (and myself) as far away from SRS as possible

"How're we doing with the recruits?" I whispered into my headset as I hurried along the hallway. I could hear voices a few halls over, but I had to trust that Ben would guide me along.

"We're loading up now!" Clatterbuck said. If all had gone according to plan, he was just outside SRS's cafeteria loading docks in a giant yellow school bus, dressed up as its driver. I wondered if Oleander had arrived in costume as well. Somehow, I doubted it.

"We're out, Hale," Kennedy said.

"Everyone's safe?" I asked.

"I'm on board," Beatrix said.

"All here, Hale," Walter said after a brief rustling from him putting his com on. "But my mom figured out that all the recruits are missing. She tried to run after us but couldn't figure out which group of cheerleaders the recruits were from the back, so I think she went to tell Fishburn and the HITS guys that she doesn't have them."

"No," Ben said. "She's actually running back to the dorms, I think. Hale, you'll have to take a left up ahead, because there's a group of senior agents at the end of the hall. They have their backs toward you, but go fast."

"Got it," I said, taking the left. I wanted to look back over my shoulder and check where the senior agents were, but no, I had to trust Ben and keep moving. I heard the bus squeal forward over my com, followed by cheering from the recruits; the sound made something in my chest melt a little. If everything else went wrong, at least we got them—and Beatrix, Walter, and Kennedy with them—out.

"Hang on, Hale, take another left here," Ben said.

"If I take a left, I go farther from the exit," I said.

"I know, but Fishburn is headed back toward his office. And then—wait, Hale. Mrs. Quaddlebaum just kicked down the door to your bedroom. She sees the BENoculars! She's—"

Ben took a sharp breath. "I've lost my feed," Ben said. His voice was dead for a second, and then he repeated himself, panicked. "I've lost my feed! Hale? She unplugged the BENoculars. I can't see the cameras anymore. I have no idea where you are or where anyone else is—"

"It's fine," I answered, even thought it wasn't. I froze in the hall and tried to listen back to the sounds of voices. *Focus, Hale,* I told myself in a voice that sounded a lot like my Dad's. I wanted to do anything *but* focus. I wanted to freak out and run and hide. But that wouldn't help me right now. Spies existed long before computers and Right Hands and cameras and BENoculars. I could do this.

I cut right, jogging down past the secretary's office. There were people in there, but they were preoccupied with sneaking up to a door in the back where I guess they thought I was hiding. More footsteps ahead, and I recognized the sound of Fishburn's fancy shoes on the tile. I hung another right and circled the hall block to pass just a few yards behind him. I could hear the breathing of my friends over the com, but no one was speaking, like they were all afraid a single sound would break my concentration. I dared to peek around another corner—there was Ms. Elma, walking my way.

"Walter, Kennedy," I whispered into the com. "I'm in the back of the admin hall. Ms. Elma is coming toward me. Fishburn is already back in his office. I need an out. Help me think." I had to move—I dropped to my knees and crawled under the Disguise Department's front window. I could hear more voices now, younger voices. The other junior agents, probably still in their SRS cheerleading uniforms, were starting to filter down to this part of the building.

"Oh, what about through the shooting range?" Kennedy asked.

"Give me the com," Oleander said, apparently snatching Kennedy's. "Hale? I'm coming in to get you."

"What? No, you'll get caught," I protested. "Don't."

"You're the most valuable asset we have, and I'm not letting you get trapped in there. I need to know exactly where you are." I heard the bus air brakes exhale over the com.

"I'm in the Disguise Department—"

"I've got an idea!" Walter interrupted, his voice a little shaky. "Dr. Oleander, don't go in after him—wait, where'd she go?"

"I'm already inside. I'll be the backup plan," Oleander whispered through her—well, Kennedy's—com. "What's your idea, Walter?"

"Okay, Hale—there's an emergency stairwell near my mom's office in the admin hall, not too far from the Disguise Department."

"What? I've never seen a stairwell there."

"You'd never know it was there if you didn't go into her office all the time—just trust me! It should be a straight shot from where you are. The door's locked, but it gives if you shove it hard enough—Cameron and Michael and I used to sneak out that way all the time. We'll park the bus right outside—just make it down the hall and up the steps. Come on!"

I paused. "I'll have to pass Fishburn's office. And there're other agents down there helping him by now, and I think a few of the junior agents would see me at the hallway intersection."

"It doesn't matter! We're *right here*. You just have to stay a little ahead of them on the stairs."

I exhaled. "I can't do that, Walter."

"What? Why not? It's perfect! Look, Clatterbuck says he and Ben put some sort of fancy engine in this bus. They'll gun it the moment that you hit the door and *boom*, we're gone. You can do it!"

"No, Walter. *You* can do it, maybe. But I won't be able to stay ahead of them on the stairs. I'm not fast enough. Hale the Whale, remember?"

I didn't want to say it out loud any more than my friends wanted to hear it. Walter made a few halted sounds like he wanted to argue, but he stopped himself. Beatrix and Clatterbuck began shouting other suggestions, panic rising in their voices. Oleander chanted over and over that I should stay put, that she was making her way to me.

I sighed and then looked down at the stack of

Groundcover papers in my hand. Once I was caught, I'd never have the chance to look. Never have the chance to learn whatever my parents had known that had forced them into hiding. Never have the chance to pass all of it along to The League, so they could stop SRS.

I couldn't escape SRS, but at least I could get some answers. I reached up and pulled the com earring off, then slipped into the archive room, where I dropped to the ground and began to read.

Project Groundcover
Mission Start Date: 01-01-84
Projected End Date: Indefinite

Objective:

Project Groundcover seeks to place young agents into deep cover across the globe, where they will be able to infiltrate government, cultural, and religious agencies, assuring SRS's control of said agencies.

[Operation Evergreen, sub-program, will seek out potential candidates for these missions, as well as replace absent SRS students who are assigned to Groundcover.]

I stared. SRS was planting kids across the world. Of course they were—it made perfect sense. It was genius, even. A few kids here and there, and boom, suddenly they controlled the planet. This was what my parents meant, when they said Project Groundcover would give SRS too much power—it would give them *all* the power, practically, and with more kids coming in through Operation Evergreen, they'd continue growing and growing until they ruled *everything*. The next few pages included maps, diagrams, blueprints, and information on the places SRS planned on sending junior agents. Then there were dozens and dozens of junior agent files, and from the looks of it, Groundcover involved kids from different SRS facilities all over the world.

Eleanor, from my class, was supposed to go to a stodgy boarding school in France, where she'd be able to befriend diplomats' children and spy on their parents. Michael would, in two years, be sent to Russia, where he'd work his way up the ranks of its navy. Walter was going to Spain, where he'd be put in place to—oh, gross—impress the president's daughter, who had a thing for shoulder muscles, and hopefully start dating her. I flipped another page and was surprised to see my own file—I guess Fishburn was serious about letting that whole physical exam thing go. It appeared I was slated to go to Norway, where I'd be . . .

I rolled my eyes. Where I'd be helping out a butler in the royal household. Walter gets a Spanish girlfriend and I get to deliver the paper. Some junior agent.

I shuffled through the papers till I got to the section where senior agents were listed. There were plenty I didn't know, but it didn't take me long to find my parents. Their sections were thick, full of long mission reports and transcripts. The cover pages were the most informative.

[Senior Agent Assignments]
Katie Jordan

Role: ~~Research~~
~~Shallow Cover - French Embassy~~
~~Shallow Cover - Home of French President~~
~~Shallow Cover - House of Lords~~
~~Shallow Cover - Russian Parliament~~
New Agent Placement

Mom was supposed to take kids and set them up in their undercover roles. No wonder she didn't like it. There was an official SRS photo of her on the last page, and underneath it, smaller photos of her in various disguises.

Joseph Jordan

Role: ~~Research~~
~~Shallow Cover - French Embassy~~
~~Shallow Cover - Home of French President~~
~~Shallow Cover - House of Lords~~
~~Shallow Cover - Russian Parliament~~
Opposition Removal

And Dad was supposed to stop anyone or anything that got in Mom's way.

I tried not to think too hard about what that might mean. I looked at Dad's photo longer than I should have, seeing as how I could still hear running in the halls, and then I turned the page.

Alex Creevy

Role: ~~Research~~
~~Shallow Cover - French Embassy~~
~~Shallow Cover - Home of French President~~
~~Shallow Cover - House of Lords~~
~~Shallow Cover - Russian Parliament~~
Deep Cover - The League

I read it again.

And again.

What?

I flipped the page, to where the photo of Alex Creevy should have been. There was a pretty woman with black hair looking back at me, though the photo looked a little old. I was surprised—Clatterbuck had made me think Alex Creevy was a man, but I suppose he'd just assumed, and Alex was one of those names that could go either way. I looked down; underneath the official photo were dozens of photos of her in disguise, just like Mom's page. Here she was as a redhead or wearing a hijab or with blue contacts in or with her eyebrows overpenciled. Here she was with blond hair.

My stomach flipped. There she was with blond hair.

I knew Alex Creevy. Only I knew her as Pamela Oleander.

CHAPTER TWENTY-SEVEN

My hands shook for a moment before I forced them to be still. How could I have missed this? There were clues, clues that screamed at me in hindsight. She hadn't just guessed the name Agent Smith in the car with Walter and me that day; she *knew* Agent Smith worked in Tactical Support. She hadn't pressed so hard about Groundcover because The League needed to know; she'd done it so she could find SRS's security weaknesses. She hadn't even asked me how to get to the Disguise Department only a few moments ago when she was breaking in to "rescue me." Why would she ask? She knew where the department was. She was an SRS agent.

"Guys, Alex Creevy. She's—"

The door to the archive slammed open. Someone punched at my arm and the com bracelet went flying. I whirled around, but another hand struck the side of my temple. It didn't knock me out, but the world went sideways for a minute, and I couldn't tell where the ground was. There were voices, I was caught, but I had to warn the others about Oleander. I mean . . . Creevy.

"You mean me," Oleander/Creevy said, and I looked up. "You were mumbling out loud. It happens sometimes with a blow to the head," she added.

"You just punched a kid in the head, Alex," someone else said. I was surprised to see Otter standing in the doorway.

"I just punched a rogue agent who is double-crossing us," Creevy corrected. Otter shrugged and collected my fallen com. Then he dropped it into his pocket and shuffled all the Groundcover papers together.

"Let's go, Jordan," Creevy said, hauling me to my feet.

"You're not really Oleander," I said dizzily. "How can you . . . How could we . . ."

"I'm very, very good at my job, that's how," Creevy said.

My vision was becoming clearer, but my mind wasn't. It felt like my entire brain had been tossed around until everything I knew was true was mixed up with everything I knew was a lie. Oleander was Creevy. Creevy was Oleander.

Villains don't always look like villains.

I felt sick.

In the hall outside the archive room were Fishburn and dozens of agents—junior and senior—staring. I couldn't get away with this many people watching, even if I could some-how overpower Creevy—who was obviously pretty willing to hurt me. Fishburn walked in front of me with Creevy and Otter just behind. Everyone was looking at me with shock and disgust, and I heard mutters like "How could you?" and "This would break your parents' hearts."

Fishburn gave his broken office window a dismayed look when we walked inside. "Ah, here we go. Agent Otter, would you mind watching the door while Agent Creevy, Hale, and I speak?" he said. His voice was still calm, like this was some sort of bizarre parent-teacher conference rather than my doom.

Otter nodded. "Yes, sir."

"Thanks for helping us find him. I can't believe you were right. I didn't peg him for a hider," Creevy said, smiling as she passed Otter. She gave him a look that made me think they didn't like each other very much, and made me know that they went way back. They were about the same age; I guessed they were in SRS classes together when they were kids.

"I've known Jordan longer than you have," Otter answered. "The key with a kid like that is remembering that he's not going to do what the other kids will do. He's not fast enough or strong enough to actually make it out of here past all the search parties we had. All he can do is hide, really."

I gave Otter the nastiest look I could muster, but I wasn't

sure how much good it did. We moved into Fishburn's office, where I was forced into the chair across from his desk, the same chair I sat in when Fishburn had told me that my parents had been compromised. I assessed the situation. Dozens of agents outside, Otter at the door, and no way to contact anyone at The League. I still had on the utility belt Ben had made for me.

Creevy reached forward and clicked the belt, then yanked it off. She tossed it to Otter in the doorway.

"Stop, Hale." Fishburn sighed at me. "I can tell you're still looking for a way out, and you know, I respect that. But stop. There are a lot of angry agents out there. Teresa Quaddlebaum alone is reason enough to stop, if you ask me."

Creevy nodded. "I'll talk to her, if you want. I think you can still get Walter back for SRS."

"What about Kennedy Jordan?" Fishburn asked.

Creevy snorted a little. "Not a chance. It's a pity too—she would've been a great junior agent."

"She would have. And plenty of those kids would have been perfect assets all over the world," Fishburn said, turning a steely eye back to me. "But now we've practically got to start over with Operation Evergreen, thanks to you, Hale. You must be feeling pretty pleased with yourself."

I firmed my jaw. "For freeing a bunch of kids you kidnapped? Yeah, I am."

Fishburn's eyes widened, like I'd said the most offensive thing possible. "Those kids would have had amazing lives! They would have become princesses and heirs and presidents! And now they're going to be, what, top chess players? Junior Olympic swimmers? The tall girl, we were going to get her married to the prince of England. Now where is she? Back to being some diplomat's boarding-school daughter?"

"You still kidnapped them," I said, ignoring Fishburn. "And you put my parents In the Weeds."

Fishburn slammed his hands down on his desk, and it took every bit of willpower I had not to jump. "Your parents were going to let everyone know about SRS. We told them what Groundcover was all about—we thought we could *trust* them—and the next thing we know, they're digging into SRS itself. This organization raised them, sheltered them, fed them, and educated their children. They're traitors." There was a pulsing vein in the middle of his forehead that reminded me of Ms. Elma's scar.

"My parents betrayed you, maybe, but they did what was right," I said.

"Abandoning you and your sister here?"

"Refusing to work for an organization of monsters. Just like I'm refusing. I quit, Fishburn. How do you like that?"

"Oh, Hale, I'm sorry, but I won't be accepting your resignation. We need you," Fishburn said. His voice made my spine crawl in the worst way.

"Whatever it is, I won't do it," I growled.

"You won't have to do much. See, we're going to hold you here to draw your parents back. We'll need to get information across the appropriate channels—Alex, write this down, please." Creevy looked annoyed at being given a job usually reserved for a secretary, but she lifted paper and a pen. "Make sure it gets out that we have the Jordans' son. Tell the Carraway brothers, MI9, the guys from Pakistan—we're willing to trade him for the two of them."

"They won't come in," I said. "But go ahead. Waste your time. Lock me up."

Creevy spoke, her voice dark. "SRS has plenty of holding cells, Hale. We can waste as much time as it takes, because they're not going to get away with this. Your parents wanted to blow a mission that's cost me ten years of my life. Steve was a shoo-in for the deep cover assignment, but then, noooo, he had to go and wreck Acapulco—"

"That wasn't my fault!" Otter snapped from the door.

"Whatever, Steve. You don't have to go back to The League, so be grateful. That whole place is one giant dead end. I can't believe we didn't realize their funding was being cut before they installed me as director. What a career-killer."

"You think Clatterbuck and the others will let you come back to The League?" I scoffed.

"You think we're going to allow you to tell them who I really am?" Creevy answered, folding her arms. I began to see just how great a spy Creevy was—because the woman in front of me was nothing at all like the Pamela Oleander I thought I knew. Her cover character was truly remarkable.

"I already told them. The minute I saw your picture. Sure, I didn't have time to go into detail, but they'll figure it out." This was a lie, of course, but I couldn't let Creevy go back to my sister and my friends.

Creevy looked at me, and I could tell she was trying to study if my pupils were dilating—one of the easiest ways to spot a lie. Mom had taught me how to keep them still, though—by breathing slowly and focusing on something close by—so in the end she looked at Fishburn for advice.

"Well, if they know, we'll have to eliminate them," Fishburn said, shrugging.

Spies were supposed to keep a cool head. We were supposed to think clearly even in the most stressful of situations.

But I basically snapped.

I lunged forward at Fishburn—to do what, exactly, I wasn't sure—but I flung myself over the desk and toward him, shouting curse words that would have gotten me grounded for years if my parents had been there. Creevy leaped at me and tried to wrestle me back into my chair, but she couldn't do it alone; Otter jumped into the office and, between the two of them, they managed to force me back down. I tried to control my breathing—I shouldn't have done that. Shouldn't have let them know they'd gotten to me.

Though, they shouldn't have threatened my little sister.

Now that he wasn't in danger of being pummeled by a twelve-year-old, Fishburn looked indignant. He smoothed his hair and glowered at me, shaking his head.

"Really, Hale? You attacked me? I guess you must really think you're something. You go on a few missions, dodge a few agents, start to feel like you're not a failure, and next thing you know, you're so arrogant that you'll attack your own director. Let me tell you something—do you think I just decided to ignore the physical requirements for fun, to give the chubby boy a chance to go on a mission or two? Don't be ridiculous. I lifted them so you'd have something to do that kept you returning to The League. I *hoped* that you'd tell Clatterbuck or 'Oleander' or even those twins something that would lead us to your parents. It wasn't because you'd earned a place on those missions, Jordan. Look at you. You're no field agent."

I didn't let my expression change. Eyes locked, mouth firm. But inside, everything felt broken. It had all been fake. Every bit of it. I wasn't ahead of them—they'd been ahead of me the entire time.

I really was trapped.

CHAPTER TWENTY-EIGHT

"Take him to holding," Fishburn said. "Both of you, just in case he gives you trouble. Don't let anyone else get close to him."

"Yes, sir," Otter said. He flung my utility belt over his shoulder, then reached forward and plucked the stack of Groundcover papers off Fishburn's desk. "I'll get these shredded too."

I rose, and Otter produced a pair of plastic handcuffs from his pocket. He looped them around my wrists, and then he and Creevy walked on either side of me through the office door. The crowd was still there, though now they were mostly silent. I didn't look at anyone's face. I had to focus on the mission. Only, there was no mission anymore. So I focused on the wall. We broke through the crowd, and they led me down several hallways, toward intake. Never had the word sounded more like "prison."

"So, Steve. What's it like being a teacher? When's the last time you went on an actual mission?" Creevy said. Her voice was teasing, but not in a fun way.

"Just the other day, actually. With Jordan. For Evergreen. He . . . well . . ." Otter cleared his throat. "He did a fine job on it. Improvised well. Surprised even me, and let's be honest—I've never liked the kid."

Creevy's voice filled with disdain. "That doesn't count. I mean a *real* mission. That hospital thing was just a distraction to make Hale feel good about himself."

"It was a real mission!" Otter said. "We had another junior agent slated to play the part before Hale turned them all purple. Which was also impressive, I have to say."

"Oh, write him a love letter already," Creevy said, rolling her eyes.

"My point is, *Alex*," Otter said, making her name sound like a bad word, "that SRS clearly trained him up well. He broke into The League, he ran point on those missions, and he broke a dozen recruits out today and got his whole team out. If you weren't an SRS agent, he'd have gotten away with it, all without passing the physical exam. That's a hell of a thing for a fat kid."

"Thanks a lot," I muttered, wishing he'd shut up. Otter shoved me in the back a little, and I tumbled, just barely catching my balance. Creevy laughed under her breath and didn't look over. Which was a good thing, because even with all the spy training in the world, I was totally incapable of hiding my surprise.

The handcuffs on my wrists weren't tight.

I only noticed because when Otter shoved me, I tried to put my hands in front of myself to keep from smashing into the ground. I hadn't needed to, but trying alone made me realize that they were big. Big enough that with a little twisting and maybe a few pinches, I'd be able to pull my hands free. Did Otter realize? I wasn't sure. Either way, I needed to wait until I had a possible exit to try anything . . . which was going to be really hard with Creevy just a half step ahead of me and Otter a step behind.

"You know, Alex," Otter spit as we took another turn, "we don't have to fight every time we're in the same room."

"We don't? But I enjoy it so much," Creevy said, flashing a smile I'd believe if I didn't know her to be totally evil on all levels.

"We don't. We've got the same goals, Alex. So we're on the same team."

I swallowed.

Because I knew then that Otter wasn't talking to Creevy. He was talking to me. My parents had said the same thing to him ages ago, back in his office. It took me a long time to process what this meant, because it seemed even more impossible than Pamela Oleander being Alex Creevy. It meant that Otter, of "Is that what you call a sit-up?" fame, was helping me.

Creevy was slowing down—we were about to take another turn, and if the giant metal door she meant to go through was any indication, this would be my final stop. She approached the door first, and when she looked down at the handle, I glanced at Otter.

He gave me the smallest of nods.

I yanked my hands from the handcuffs in one swoop. Otter dropped my utility belt and the Groundcover papers and dived for Creevy, who immediately began to fight him off. Otter was quick, though, and he held his own against her. I dropped to the ground and grabbed my belt and as many of the Groundcover papers as I could. The alarm began to sound again, even shriller down here in the land of tile floors and heavy doors—they'd spotted us on the cameras.

"Go!" Otter grunted at me, reaching into his pocket and flinging my com unit at me. Creevy kicked him in the stomach and lunged for me, but I ducked and set her flying over my head. She rebounded, but Otter cut her off again. She was in better shape—it wouldn't be long before she got the best of him.

Otter was going to pay for this. As often as I'd wanted to make him pay, I couldn't be happy about that.

But I ran. I raced down the hall the way we came, lungs tightening and muscles begging for rest. There was the heavy door, probably with agents on the other side. I clipped on my utility belt as I huffed along, then jammed my com back onto my ear just as I heard the sound of Creevy's heels on tile, racing after me.

"Ben! Ben, are you there?" I wheezed into the com.

"Hale!" Ben shouted triumphantly, and I heard cheering. "You're alive!"

"For now—I'm trying to get out. What does the Hell-BENder do?"

"Huh?"

"The HellBENder! I'm about to run into the SRS hall, alone, and that's the only thing I've got left. You said it was a last resort"—I had to stop to take a big gulp of air—"but I can't use it if it's going to blow up the building or kill everyone or something—"

"Hale, again with the dark stuff. Do you seriously think I'd invent something—"

"What does it do?" I said, hacking into the earring. The door was growing closer. There wasn't any time to stop and talk this through, not with the sound of Creevy bearing down on me.

"Take it," Ben said confidently. "Just take it. It's a last resort, but don't worry. We'll be here to get you when it wears off, so long as you can make it out of the building."

I had no idea what he meant. I didn't even see how I could take something that looked like a tube of lipstick. But I reached down for my belt and plucked the HellBENder off, and then I pulled the cap off the tube. Sure enough, what looked like lipstick turned out to be a single fat pill. I lifted it to my mouth as I hit the door that led into the hall.

Agents. Senior agents, not junior ones. Staring at me, fingers flexed, heads down, wearing sleek black SRS uniforms.

I swallowed the HellBENder.

I didn't know how I knew this, but I was pretty sure that the moment the HellBENder took effect felt exactly like what eating the sun would feel like.

My whole body was energy. All of it. It was like my chest was full of sun and volcanoes. Suddenly my lungs didn't seem too small—they seemed too *big*. Adrenaline raced through me in ways I'd never known. I tossed a handful of the Groundcover papers at the senior agents and then barreled through them. They lashed out at me, kicking, punching, backflipping, but I forged ahead, strength I'd never known blasting through me.

A few more agents were in front of me, racing to get down to where the alarms were sounding. They braced themselves, but I was past them before they realized what was happening. I threw another handful of papers in the air at them and kept moving. The elevators would be shut down, but the garage exits might still be open. I flew toward the cafeteria, ignoring the faces of my classmates, my teachers, the very confused HITS guy that I was passing . . .

Ben was suddenly in my ear again. "Hale, hurry. By my watch you've only got a few seconds left!"

"Till what?" I shouted back.

"Go!" Ben roared, and now he sounded scared. I finally threw the final handful of Groundcover papers over my head. They rained down behind me like confetti. It wasn't the neatest way to try to tell people about Groundcover, but it would work. At least, I hoped it would. Surely, if news of me doing an impression of Mrs. Quaddlebaum could get around in an hour, news that SRS was kidnapping kids and trying to kill off their own agents could get around even faster? I threw my weight against the doors to the garage and ran past sports cars and trucks and a tank some department was refurbishing.

The garage doors. They were being lowered, slowly. I only had a few seconds to get to them before this exit would be useless. I squeezed my eyes shut and somehow, impossibly, sped up. It felt like every cell in my body was exploding, every bit of blood was hot and angry. The crack of sunlight under the garage grew slimmer, slimmer, slimmer . . .

I flung myself at the ground and tumbled out into the sun.

I was out.

But I also couldn't move. There were footsteps, footsteps I wanted to run from but couldn't because suddenly my arms weighed entirely too much for me to lift. But then Clatterbuck and Walter were lifting me up, running with me. There was the school bus, and there was Kennedy.

And then there was just blackness.

CHAPTER TWENTY-NINE

"Hale! Do! You! Hear! Me!"

Yes. I hear you. Stop yelling. I was trying really hard to say that out loud, but it wasn't working.

"I think he's in shock."

"He's not in shock."

"He might be in shock."

"You don't know."

"Guys, be quiet. I think he's waking up."

"He can't wake up; he's in shock. What'd you put in that thing?"

"It's sort of a super-adrenaline spike. So you burn fast, but short. That's why it's a last resort. I used all the caffeine I could legally buy."

"I'm in shock."

"See! I told you he was in shock!"

It took me a moment to realize I'd finally said something out loud. I winced and opened my eyes very, very slowly. The twins, Kennedy, and Walter were gathered around me, and the overhead lights were incredibly bright. Or so they seemed, anyway. It took only a moment for them to fade into regular gym lights. We were back at League head-quarters.

"Seriously," I said, "I'm in shock. What happened?"

Walter answered first. "You passed out. We got you. We brought you here. But you've been totally out for almost a day and a half. Kennedy's the one who drew the unicorns on your arm—"

"What about Creevy?" I felt frantic, like my mind was still all HellBENdered but my body wasn't listening. "Oleander—she's Creevy—"

"We know, Hale. We know everything. Hey, I think you should eat something. That should help you feel normal faster," Ben said.

"Did it help when you tested the HellBENder?" Beatrix asked as Walter helped me stand. Ben didn't answer, which told me he hadn't actually tested it. That wasn't surprising.

What was surprising, however, was what I saw when we got to the cafeteria. There, eating a sandwich with Clat-terbuck, was Agent Otter. He looked thoroughly disgusted by the entire place and kept inspecting his bread as if he thought he'd find mold on it. Walter helped me limp over to him; he didn't look up till I was only a few feet away.

There were a lot of things I wanted to say, but I settled for the thing begging to be asked. "How did you get out?"

Otter gave me a sour look, like he was really very annoyed that I was conscious again. "I took a page out of the Hale Jordan book and cheated. They chased after me, and I took them out one by one using whatever I could find. Took a few shortcuts, threw around a few empty water jugs. Beat them to the door by a hair, but they didn't want to risk exposing the facility by chasing me into the street."

"I don't cheat," I said, because I had to make sure that was clear, but I smiled at him a little. I expected Otter to sort of smile back, maybe because we'd pretty much been through a lot together at that point. Instead he scowled, threw his sandwich into its plastic wrap, and walked away.

"Huh," Beatrix said, watching him go.

"You get used to him after a while. A long while," Walter assured her. He handed me a different sandwich, and we sat down. Well. *They* sat down—I sort of slumped into my chair uselessly.

"Who else is here?" I asked. "Other than Otter? I threw as many of those papers out as I could, but I don't know how many people saw them."

Kennedy and Walter looked at each other a little nervously. "No one," Kennedy finally answered. "*Yet.* Leaving SRS will be hard for them, Hale. Maybe they'll need more convincing than we did." She gave Walter a pitying look as she said this—this meant his mom was still back at SRS.

"But," Walter said, like he was trying to look on the bright side, "all the recruits are on their way back to their homes. And we figured out Groundcover."

"So that means . . ." I looked over at Kennedy. "Mom and Dad can come home."

She nodded at me, beaming, and then did a walkover out of her chair.

"They're going to hear about it any day now, don't you think? I mean, I know they're lying low, but I'm sure they're still keeping up with things. I bet by Friday," she said as she righted herself.

Friday came. Friday went. Our parents still hadn't contacted us.

The League, however, had a very good week. Not only did the government give them all sorts of funding back—they had, after all, stopped an SRS world takeover—but they named a new director: Agent Otter. I wasn't saying they chose him because he was literally the only choice available, but . . . he was literally the only choice available. Also, he needed a job, and it was hard for a former spy from a top-secret organization to just get a job at a sandwich shop or something.

"What do you expect me to do, Jordan?" he snapped at me. We were in his office. Amazingly, he'd managed to make it Otter-y in a matter of hours. Gone were Oleander's orchids and pictures of sunsets. In their place were already-dying houseplants and empty nail hooks.

"The League just got all sorts of funding back! I expect you to use that money to help find my parents."

"Just got funding back after years and years of *nothing*. The government wants us to take out SRS, one mission at a time, but we don't even have a decent computer. We definitely have to buy new servers. And we have to somehow recruit and train new agents—other than Clatterbuck, who, let's face it, isn't exactly a shining example of a spy, there's not another agent in this entire building."

"There's me. And Walter. And Kennedy. And Beatrix and Ben, even if they aren't field agents."

"You are not a junior agent," Otter said, pointing a finger at me.

"Will you *get over that stupid physical exam*?" I yelled—really, yelled—and leaned over the desk. "It's just a pointless test! I'm a good field agent, Otter; you know I am! What am I going to have to do to prove it to you?"

"The physical exam!" Otter yelled back, waving his hands at how obvious this was.

I clenched my fists. "Look, believe me—*believe me*—I did not think we'd end up having to work together. I thought I'd leave SRS, and Mom and Dad would come home, and to be honest, I never thought for a second what would happen to you because . . . whatever. But here we are. I'm not asking you to pay me—I'm not asking you to even be nice to me—but I am asking you to *help me find my parents*."

I sat back down. It felt like I was experiencing some sort of anger high, and it took a few moments for me to stop shaking.

Otter seemed to be experiencing the same thing. He rolled his tongue around his mouth for a while and then balanced his pencil on its tip. Finally he reached into his drawer and pulled out a newspaper, which he dropped on the table in front of me.

"Here. I don't know what it is, but I think it's for you."

Then he got up to leave the office. Just after he passed me, he stopped and spoke without looking at me. "It's not a pointless test, Jordan, any more than the other junior agent tests are. It's there to keep you safe. To prove that when it all goes down in the field, you'll be able to make it out alive. I don't like you, Jordan, but that doesn't mean I want to send you off to get killed."

I waited a moment, considering this. He was right. I knew that. And yet . . .

"Don't worry about me getting killed, Agent Otter. My friends wouldn't let that happen."

Otter made a gruff sort of noise and then left his office. I thought I heard him muttering something about entitlement in the hall.

I opened the newspaper carefully and went to the classifieds. I knew exactly where to look, because a half dozen ads had been circled and then crossed out—I guess Otter was looking for codes or ciphers in them. One ad was simply circled, an ad for a lost pet. It read:

LOST hedgehog. Answers to Tinsel.
$1,523 reward
646-961-4253 for more info.

I was holding my breath, but it wasn't until I had to gasp for air that I realized it. This was a message for me, all right. If the hedgehog named Tinsel were there alone, I might get worried it was some sort of SRS trick, but there was the code, our code—1523, my birthday and Kennedy's birthday together. I grabbed the phone—it was taupe—off Otter's desk and frantically dialed the number.

It rang. It rang a thousand times, it felt like, before finally there was a click, and it went to voice mail.

"Hi, Hale and Kennedy," my mom's voice said, and I closed my eyes. I hadn't heard her voice in a long time. *"We know you've been waiting to hear from us, and we're sorry it has to be over a voice mail like this. We're so proud of both of you. Hale, what you pulled off at SRS . . . Well . . . we always believed in you, but you took 'believe' to a whole new level. Groundcover is dead, at least for now—SRS won't risk putting any more agents on it since you and The League could expose them. And I know you think that means your dad and I will get to come home.*

"I wish it were that simple. But the truth is, Groundcover

was just the biggest project we knew about. When we suspected SRS wasn't exactly what they'd always told us, we started investigating, and, guys, it's bigger than one project. There are hundreds of agents, hundreds of missions, and hundreds of SRS facilities, and not one of them is up to any good.

"Right now you're safe at The League because SRS is afraid if they hurt you two, your father and I will retaliate and expose them. If we came there, though, they'd have everyone capable of exposing them under one roof. SRS has always been hesitant to attack The League outright, what with them being in the middle of a city and all, but all of us together . . . I'm not sure they'd be able to ignore that.

"What I'm saying, Hale, Kennedy, is that we're safe. And you're safe. And we love you, and we're glad to see you working with The League—though I did hear that Steve is running that show now, so sorry about that. But we can't come back to you just yet, which . . . Well, it's hard for me to even say that out loud, because I know how much you both wanted it. Dad and I wanted it too.

"We'll keep an eye on you two, and the moment it's safe to come home, we will. In the meantime stick with The League. They were the only spy organization ever brave enough to stand up to SRS, and I think with a little work, they can be great again.

"We have to go—we bounced this call off a mess of different servers, but someone can probably trace it if we're here longer than two and a half minutes. So be safe, be strong, and remember to be careful out there. We love you."

She sniffed, and I heard my dad say something in the background, though I couldn't tell what. And then she hung up.

A prompt asked me if I wanted to repeat the message. I did. Again and again, until I could recite it pretty much by heart. Without meaning to, I began analyzing where I thought the call came from. There was a car engine in the background, something loud, and I thought I heard a bird . . . If I could work out what sort of bird, and cross-reference that with car models popular in different areas . . .

No.

They were right. It wasn't safe for them to come back yet.

So I hung up the phone.

CHAPTER THIRTY

Mission: Become a Superspy
Step 1: Find an acceptable home base

"Where did you *find all this*?" Kennedy squealed. Seriously, she squealed. Her voice sounded like car tires did right before they gained traction.

It was endearing.

"This store at the mall. Ben and Beatrix wouldn't go in with me," Clatterbuck said, giving them a dark look.

"I could smell the pink. I'm serious. You could actually *smell* pink," Ben said. Beatrix nodded in agreement.

We were in Kennedy's bedroom—her new bedroom, which was one of the League dorms. It had a pink rug, a pink bedspread, and so many kitten cheerleading posters on the wall that it looked like she was building a kitten army.

It wasn't exactly like her room in our apartment back at SRS, but it was close.

"Look, I put this in," Ben said, and he pulled a purple lever beside the door. The mattress rose and flopped over on its side. I thought something had gone wrong for a second, but then it flopped open again, and I realized it had turned itself into a tumbling mat. Kennedy reached levels of excitement that only dogs could hear, and hugged Ben and then Beatrix and then Clatterbuck and then me and then Walter, who hadn't had anything to do with this stuff and was really confused by all the pink.

"And I'm here," Beatrix explained, pointing to the room next to Kennedy's, "and then Ben, then Hale, then Walter, and then Uncle Stan is going to be at the front of the hall. And then Otter said he's just going to sleep three floors up because he's afraid we'll bother him at night."

"What, you mean, like, if we snore?" Clatterbuck asked.

"No—he said it would bother him if we were alive at night," Beatrix answered, shrugging.

We were all moving into League headquarters. It just made sense, really—Walter, Kennedy, and I wouldn't fit into the apartment that the twins and Clatterbuck used to live in, and Otter couldn't go far since he was the director now. Most of the other staff—the handful of computer researchers Kennedy and I had tied up the first day, and the receptionist—weren't staying here, but I hoped that before too long there'd be other field agents moving into the empty rooms. It'd be a long time before The League had numbers that compared to SRS but . . . The League had us.

Well, actually, The League basically *was* us.

"Come on," Clatterbuck said after Kennedy folded and refolded her bed/tumbling mat a few more times. "We have a briefing on the deck."

"Really?" Walter asked.

"That's what Director Otter said," Clatterbuck said. We walked together to the deck, which still looked shabby compared to SRS's, but it was really coming along. Otter had had the whole thing painted a sleek gray, and there was new carpet. Plus, the stations now had real office chairs at them instead of cafeteria chairs Ben and Clatterbuck had originally stolen. Otter was standing in the back, looking through a stack of papers.

Step 2: Organize and define operations

"What's up?" I asked.

"I've put together everything I can remember from my last few missions at SRS. They were a while ago, since I've been teaching you people for the past five years, but it's something. There's one in particular I thought we should check out as our first mission. There's the case name at the top—pull it up on your machine . . . thing . . . That hand thing . . ." he said to Beatrix, and gave her one of the documents.

"Right Hand," Walter corrected him. Otter rolled his eyes.

"Why this one?" Beatrix asked as she typed a few things into her Right Hand. The enormous screen in front of us clicked on and was soon displaying a variety of pictures and documents that seemed to depict a bank. A Swiss bank, if I had to guess.

"Because it's the one I chose, and I'm the director," Otter said. When we all lifted our eyebrows in near unison, he exhaled. "And because if we pull this off, we crack into SRS's funding, which is a pretty great first strike. Besides, we bankrupt them, and we can afford to hire some cafeteria workers. Okay?"

I looked at the others. "Well. Let's do it then."

Step 3: Get to work